AFTER THE BEFORE

ERNIE GAMMAGE

First Edition, 2025
ISBN: 979-8-9926982-1-3 (paperback)

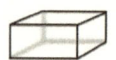

Austin, Texas

To my children and their children and their children and
Stephanie.

In time,
Who knows what comfortable cottages
Can be built on the snouts of dragons?
In time.

Ernie

1

"Got it!" Markus said. "I got it."

"What is it?" Sophie called back.

"Not sure, but it's hard. Has corners. A box."

Markus pushed in deeper past his elbow, fingers digging into the muck. He was on the wall of a crater in what had once been a mountain of trash, the remains of centuries-old detritus from The Before. A fresh rainstorm had exposed some of what he'd hoped to find, something of value. It was after these rains that scavenging was best.

Up above on the rim, Sophie dug in her feet and pulled against the rope tied to Markus below. She yelled down, "Watch it, Markus! This is all the rope I've got. Slip any more, and we'll both be in trouble." Sturdy, Sophie easily anchored these trips into the craters and had no trouble keeping Markus from sliding down their sides. Sweat gleamed on her clear high forehead, and she brushed at the stray hair that stuck to her, orphans from the pale braid that hung down her back. Her blue eyes were intent.

"Yeah, I know. I'm being careful. There's…something…in here. I can feel it, can almost get my hand around it." He thrust further into the side of the crater, cheek pressed against the muck.

Markus was a few years younger (he thought) than Sophie. They'd been together since they were abandoned as children, passed around to strangers and occasional relatives. Their histories were full of holes. Now, both in their twenties, their relationship had become less clear. Was she his workmate? Sister? Girlfriend?

Sophie leaned over the crater's edge, as close as she dared, until the ground began to break loose. The garbage mountains were always ready to crumble, but in them were things for barter and sale. It was how they survived. She leaned back, straining against the rope, forehead furrowed with effort. The work had made her strong and lean.

While Markus was tasked with finding the things they bartered, it was Sophie who evaluated worth, cut the deals, and haggled over fair value. They were a good team: she had her job; he had his.

"I'm coming up!" Markus called, clutching the dirty box under his arm. He was slim and wiry, deeply tanned, with sun-washed dark curly hair that hung to his shoulders. A sharp nose and gray eyes gave him a hawkish appearance. "Hold firm, Sophie." She shoved her heels into the dirt, bracing against his weight, and Markus crawled up and out, holding his prize. He was filthy, but that came with the job—that, and the rancid odor from the pit. "Here, take this," he said, trading the box for the rope, which he coiled neatly.

"It's plassik!" Sophie shook the box, wiping crud from its flat, translucent surfaces. It was small enough to carry, but large enough to be unwieldy.

"Let's see," said Markus, reaching for it. "What's inside? Something…" He turned the box this way and that, looking for an entry point. There wasn't one. "Let's take it back to Jen's and see if she can open it."

They changed into fresher clothes and set off from the pit across the crater-pocked plain. Of all the craters, the one they'd been in was the only one in the trash mountain, the only one exposing its wealth. The cratered landscape stretched far beyond them to the City. Its bombardment, and everything around it so long ago, had ravaged the plain.

"We may have hit a jackpot, Sophie…well, maybe a little jackpot," said Markus, smiling as he reached over to clutch Sophie's shoulder. They'd been at this a long time, and these kinds of finds were rare.

"Hope so. We need it," she said as they entered the woodland.

A wide space framed by oaks and elms opened the worn path to Jen's Place, the encampment deep in the woodland that had grown from a small camp to a village over the years. Here and there among the trees were lean-tos, a well, fire pits for cooking, a weaver's loom, laundry tubs with drying racks for clothes, storage sheds, and even a small amphitheater for gatherings.

Sophie and Markus trudged along the path. Soon they smelled wood-fire smoke from the camp. "This could be our biggest find in…I don't know how long. The box alone could be worth a lot, especially something this big. And whatever's inside…" said Sophie. "I hope Jen can open it."

The amphitheater in Jen's Place was on the edge of the village, a clearing in the trees. Jen sat in a large chair crafted of bent and entwined branches. A small deep-caramel woman of indeterminate age, Jen wore graying hair that hung lank to her waist. It was interwoven with bits of colored ribbon, treasures from the trash mountains. She wore little jewelry but sported multiple red and black tattoos on her arms and up her neck. Her eyes were a remarkable piercing blue-green caused, they said, by exposure to the miasma from the pits. Regardless of the cause, those eyes had earned her fame and respect.

Barth stood by her side. He was as big a man as anyone had seen and not one to trifle with. His long red beard made him look even more fearsome. Whether she needed his protection was debatable, but she got it nevertheless.

People milled around Jen as Markus and Sophie approached. Eying the box, those nearest Jen backed away, aware there was novelty afoot. Jen greeted them with a nod. "Markus, Sophie. What have we here?"

"Not sure," Markus answered, "but we think it's plassik. There's something inside." He rattled it and handed it to her. "We can't open it. Can you?"

Jen took the box, shook it, and brushed away more of the now-dried crud. With a fingernail, she scraped the surface of the box and held it up to the light.

"Yes, something's in here all right, and the box seems to be plassik. At this size, it could be worth more than a bit. Barth, give me your knife."

The big man stood motionless, eyes elsewhere.

"Barth!" Jen said sharply.

Shaking his head with a blink, Barth glanced at Jen, took the knife from his scabbard, and handed it over. Jen took it and worked the blade at the box's edges where a seam should be, all to no avail. She bent closer, scraping again at the dried grime to get a clearer look at what was inside. It was flat, the size of two splayed hands, and could be blue or green. Through the translucent plassik, she couldn't tell.

"Barth, see if you can do any better."

Barth took the box in his large hands and felt for

an edge, something to hold on to while he pried the box apart. There was nothing.

"I can break it open if you like," he said. "I think I probably can."

Jen said, "No, what's inside might be the real prize here. Looks like…I don't know. Whatever it is, I don't want to ruin it." She paused, taking back the box, studying it. She twisted the box this way and that, lips pursed. "If there's anyone who can open this, it will be Albright. He needs to see this and what's inside. I think he might be *very* interested in what's in here." There was more than one reason to see Albright. It was time.

Markus and Sophie looked at each other, smiling. Albright! That meant a trip to the City. "Really?" asked Markus. "When do you want to leave?"

As Jen got up from her chair, handing the box back to Markus, she said, "Soon. Tomorrow."

Sophie and Markus had been to the City as children, traveling with a family that had taken them in. They remembered only the gaunt nubs of buildings, the scurrying of feral creatures, and the uneasy feeling of unseen eyes. It had not been a pleasant place for children. For Jen to invite them to travel there now was an honor and a break from scavenging the pits.

That night they slept in one of the lean-tos near the center of the village. Even in the woodland, it got cold at night, and they snuggled together for warmth under a rabbit-hair blanket. Markus, lying wide-eyed in the dark, said, "Do you think Albright can open the box and figure out what's in it? What do you think it is?"

Sophie rolled over. "Go to sleep, Markus! It's been a long day. We'll talk tomorrow." Markus snuggled closer, and she moved away, but not far.

Markus lay there, eyes still open. Thinking about the day's find, he drifted back to the day a half-dozen years ago that had ended very differently…

Sophie yelled as the rope snapped and she plunged face-first down into the pit. Markus almost followed her but grabbed a steering wheel embedded in the wall of the crater. Sophie had no such luck and tumbled to the bottom.

"Sophie! You okay? Sophie?"

Nothing.

"Hold on. I'm coming down." He tied the trailing rope to the steering wheel, tugging first to gauge if it would hold him, and belayed to the bottom of the pit.

She lay crumpled on her side in the slimy muck. "Sophie…talk to me. You okay?"

Sophie rolled to her back and moaned. Bone stuck out of her left forearm at a distressing angle. She opened her eyes. "Wow. That was…something," she said. Then she saw her arm and shrieked.

With difficulty, Markus got her to the top of the crater and to the healer's place in the village. By the end of the next day, her arm was red with infection from the muck.

He sat beside her; she was hot to the touch. Opening her eyes, she turned to him.

"Hi."

He took a hand in both of his and said, "You're gonna be okay. *We're* gonna be okay."

The smell of breakfast meat pulled Sophie awake. Adjusting her gray shift, she stepped out of the lean-to into the clear morning light. Birds chirped softly in the branches above. Other voices drifted through the trees, hushed in the early morning. Sophie slipped into her shoes—soft, heelless, muddy from the day before—and headed to the fire.

Jen was up, working a cookfire with a stick. A few others milled around. One thing about Jen, she always looked composed. She never got riled, never got angry—not that she'd never had good reason to. She was simply that way. That's why this was Jen's Place.

"Oh, you're up. Where's Markus?" she said, glancing at Sophie and poking the fire, smoke rising into the sharp morning air. "Here." She handed Sophie a wooden plate heaped with scraps of steaming meat and two squares of hard bread.

"Still asleep." She picked up a strip of meat and dropped it into her mouth, chewing. "Jen, how long will it take us to get to the City? Markus and I passed through there when we were small, but I don't remember much about the trip."

"It might take a week, maybe more, depending. Traveling on the plain is never easy, and the foothills can be rough as well. Why do you ask?" She raked the fire with her stick, sending sparks flying.

"I don't know what it is, but I've been feeling… restless, I guess. Markus and I traveled so much when we were kids, landing here—the village—growing up here; that's the best thing that's happened to us. I love it here, but I'm ready for something new. Maybe this trip is it." She swung her thick braid behind her and took another bite. "What are the people who live there like? Does Albright live there by himself?"

"Questions, questions. We'll have plenty of time to talk about Albright and the City." Jen nudged the fire, jabbed her firestick into the ground, and turned to appraise Sophie. "Sophie, you and Markus have been together for as long as I've known you. I wonder…have you and he been intimate? And if you have, are you being careful?"

A square of bread slid off Sophie's plate.

2

Sophie, Markus, Jen, and Barth left the woodland after breakfast. Besides the plassik box, they brought plump water bags and the hard bread the woodland cooks baked. Barth was with them for two good reasons. The way between Jen's Place and the City was long and peopled by scavengers, thieves, and worse. Clothed in hard-earned hides—some stiff like armor—and armed with a crossbow, he would keep them safe, and if there was game, he'd bring it to the fire.

Jen led, stabbing the ground with her walking stick. "Barth, take care now. It will be a while before we can stop," she yelled over her shoulder. Their water and food would get them almost as far as the City. They'd need to find something to hunt along the way, critters from The Before, changed but still good roasted over an open fire. Their journey would take them through country that, even when quiet, hummed with the past. Eons ago, the plain was the floor of a shallow ocean that lapped on the plateau on which the City sat.

As they zigzagged between craters large and small, Sophie asked, "Jen, did you know Albright when he was young? I've heard his name but don't know anything about him. What's he like?"

"Yes, I knew him before he moved to the City, back when he camped not far from the woodland. I'd just found the place and had moved there; others followed. One day he showed up and then kept showing up. We couldn't get a good read on him. He was as commanding as anyone I'd ever met. Still, something was a little intimidating about him, something a little 'off.' It never felt like he wanted to belong there. He was always looking past the horizon, if you know what I mean.

"I think he warmed to me, though it was hard to tell. I must admit I found him attractive—we were both young, remember—but he wasn't interested in me in the way I became interested in him."

Sophie blushed, trying to imagine Jen "interested" and what that might entail. She couldn't picture it— or didn't want to.

"He did tell me before he left for the City that he was leaving. Didn't have to, of course, and I took that as a sign that at least he had some respect for me. He talked about the end of The Before, finding out what caused it and why. Said he'd find 'more' there in the City. One thing I know, he's smart, smarter than anyone I've ever met. He'll figure out how to open your box and where to find a buyer for the plassik and whatever's inside."

There was little to see: uneven ground, the occasional low scrub, withered grass, and unending craters. Jen stopped them once to eat and drink and they moved on.

"Jen, what's with Barth?" Sophie whispered as they moved around a wide crater. "I don't know if I've ever heard him talk. Does he talk?"

"Barth is…different, different from you and me, Sophie. He's been with me for a long time; we don't need to talk. I'd trust him with my life, *have* trusted him with my life. More than once. Be glad we have him with us."

Sophie glanced back over her shoulder. "I am."

Jen was quiet for a moment, then while glancing at Sophie said, "You also need to know something else about Barth. He has a gift, the gift of foretelling, passed down through his family for generations."

Sophie was wide-eyed. She'd heard of those who had visions but had never met anyone with that gift.

"I tell you this because it's your first time being around him. When he goes to that place, his visions, it's like he's in a trance. What he sees most times are mysteries to him. They have to be studied to be explained. Just know they can be very useful. As I said, he's different from us."

That night, they sidestepped down the slope of a crater to camp. Their firelight would be less visible than up on the plain, and there was no reason to attract unwanted attention. Barth produced a flint and steel, and up top they gathered dry grass. There were no trees on the plain, but the roots of a dark-red, leafless shrub burned hot and long. Jen and Barth camped on one side of the fire, Sophie and Markus on the other. Despite the fire, by morning Sophie and Markus awoke huddled together.

After a small, cold breakfast, they moved on toward the faraway City.

By Jen's reckoning, it would take five days to get to the foothills of the plateau, then another two or three until they reached the City. She looked over her shoulder at those behind her. "Markus, pick it up, will you? We want to get to the City sooner than later."

Jen stopped, planted her walking stick in the sand, and held up her hand. "Wait. Listen."

Except for the wind, it was quiet. Then they heard it: faint, metallic, mechanical, like a wonky tricycle ridden too fast.

She spoke in a whisper, remaining still, listening. "If it's A-Eye, we're in for it. Quick." Jen signaled for them to follow her down into the crater behind them.

Like many of the plain's craters, it was wide and deep, deep enough to hide them. Barth helped her descend the steep and disintegrating talus. Markus took Sophie's hand, and together they sidestepped to the bottom. Jen put her finger to her lips, whispering, "Shhhhh."

At the crater's bottom, Barth slowly turned, eyes on the edge above, crossbow raised. Sophie and Markus stood back-to-back. Jen picked at a silver necklace hanging from her neck, head cocked to one side, listening. Even from the bottom of the crater, they still heard it, a faint mechanical sound. They waited.

Long after they could no longer hear the metallic grinding, they stayed put. The sun arced over the crater; shadows moved from one side to the other. Jen nodded to Barth, and he began a slow crawl up to the crater's edge. There he stopped, and after a moment he waved for the others to follow. Sophie took Jen's arm and patiently helped her sidestep up the side of the crater. Markus followed with water bags and the box. At the top they stood, scanning the horizon.

"Were those A-Eye?" asked Sophie.

"I think so, yes," said Jen. "Can't mistake that sound."

"Are they hunting us?" Sophie clutched her shift.

"Probably. It's hard to say what they'll do. They've changed. There are more of them now, and they're more aggressive than they used to be. They've figured out how to replicate themselves. At least that's what people think."

"Why haven't we had trouble with them in the woodland? Have they ever attacked the village?" asked Markus.

"No," said Jen. "They haven't, and I don't know why. My best guess is that the forest disrupts some basic function, and they can't operate in the woodland. That sounds unlikely, but something's keeping them away or has so far."

"I've heard about them all my life, but I don't really know what they are," said Sophie. "Every story I've heard has been different."

"They're mechanical, created during The Before, and somehow became sentient," said Jen. "Once that happened and they escaped into the world, that was the end of The Before. At least that's one story. The other story, if you can believe it, is they're from somewhere out there." She looked up at the blank gray sky. "Descendants of the beings that caused The After.

"Whichever story is true, they're devils on Earth with a taste for meat. It doesn't make sense since they're machines, but because of that, some believe the story that they are descendants of aliens."

Jen paused. "All this is just what I've heard over the years. What really happened, the details of it all? Well, there's no one alive now who knows. There was a thing called Hisry, stories written down for people to look at when they wanted to know what happened in the past. After The Before, there was no more Hisry. It all disappeared, and the people who knew the Hisry, they're long gone. Long, long gone."

She stopped, lost in thought. "A few people—Albright's one of them—have tried to retrieve Hisry, figure out what The Before was like, who or what caused The After. He might be able to answer some of these questions. I can't."

3

There were three of them, all the color of the earth, stooped as they walked; one dragged his foot. Dust trailed their footsteps as they wove around the craters. Frenz led the other two. Weathered, his beard speckled with gray, he was still fit. Everything he wore had been scavenged: thick boots, the belt, scabbard, and knife; even his clothes—a tunic and leggings of rough gray homespun. The tallest of the three, he kept a wary eye out, head bobbing from the beaten ground to the horizon and back.

The other two were little more than dead weight, but they brought a certain amount of heft to his endeavors, something he needed. Shambling over the empty terrain, they'd traveled for longer than usual but had found nothing of worth or anything to eat. Frenz recognized the look in the eyes of his companions: hunger.

He despised being driven by hunger. Desperation fueled mistakes, bad decisions. Trudging along, he thought back to when his pack had numbered five...

It was a day not unlike this. He and his pack—that's how he thought of them—had walked long and hard, with little to show for it. The sun was setting. They were all hungry. Frenz, Big Rod, Capper, Mutt, and Pisser, all hungry.

As usual, Frenz took the lead as they walked. A glint caught his eye, and he nudged Mutt. "You see that? Up there?"

Mutt, whose eyes were not the best, squinted in the direction Frenz had pointed. He shook his head.

"Up *there.*" He pointed. "Pisser, you see it, don't you? Up there! A light, a little one, not big enough for a fire." Saying those words set his mouth watering. Fire meant food. "You and Mutt slide up there and take a look, okay?"

"Could be a low star, couldn't it? I don't see nothing." Pisser stood on his toes to get a better look. He was short to begin with, and pitiful nutrition had stunted and bent him more. He wiped his stringy beard.

"I still don't see nothing, but we'll go have a look-see. Better than just walking. C'mon, Mutt." They moved toward where Frenz had pointed, splitting up to be on either side of the crater in front of them.

Frenz stood in the dusk, watching them disappear over a low hill. His mouth still watered, although he was certain the light was not a fire. He waited. Big Rod and Capper fidgeted beside him, Capper favoring his bum leg. They kept their mouths shut so they wouldn't pull some godforsaken duty.

Then they heard the howls. Human. Frenz eyed them both, tipped his head toward the sound. They took off at a trot, or as much of one as age and health allowed, climbing a small hill. From the higher ground, Frenz surveyed the landscape. Nothing. No one. No Mutt. No Pisser. And no evidence of a fire. He was sure he'd seen a light but wondered, *Was it A-Eye?* He shivered. "Let's get out of here."

At the edge of a crater, they lay about clutching their water bags. Dark had descended, and they had begun to feel safe. At least they hadn't seen anyone or anything else. Mutt and Pisser: they were surely eaten or dead or both. Frenz was certain now it had been the A-Eye, and he'd sent his men to certain death. Because they were hungry.

A-Eye. When he'd first moved here, down from the perpetual snow, the first people he met told him about them. Frenz had laughed: *Armed sentient killing machines that roam the countryside in packs? You have to be kidding, right?* Then, months later on a foray, he topped a hill—far enough away to be safe—and saw what had been described to him: three very large man-like machines ripping the meat from two scavengers. Then eating it. He'd never forgotten that.

After walking for the rest of the afternoon, they settled down for the night, Frenz taking first watch on the edge of a crater, Capper and Big Rod below. He glanced at them as they slept, all that now remained of his pack. *This isn't what I wanted…to be responsible for them, to be relied on. No one should depend on me. Ever.* But they did, and he knew it. And even though he didn't like to admit it, he needed them as much as they needed him. In this country, the odds were better for three than one alone.

But what to do now? They'd all begun to weaken; it had been two days since they'd eaten, although they still had water. They could last until it ran out, then that was it. He was kneeling, scratching in the dirt with a stick, when he saw it.

It was hard most of the time to determine what was scuttling in and out of the craters, what it had been before. There were some creatures that still resembled their native forms. A snake was still usually long and serpentine, regardless of how many eyes, mouths, or even limbs it had. Most avians still resembled the birds they had once been. At least if it had but two legs, it would most likely be some kind of bird.

For everything else, though, it was anyone's guess. What now bolted in and out of a small, shallow crater was one of those.

Frenz reached down beside him, feeling for the

crossbow he carried, and found it, loaded and cocked. He never took his eyes off whatever-it-was. What it was didn't matter because they'd eat it, regardless. He pulled the crossbow beside him, up and in front.

Fifteen meters away, the thing moved, nosing into the dirt. It was large enough to feed the three of them, Frenz figured, but not so large it would present a problem if he only wounded it. He had one bolt in the crossbow and needed to make this shot count. And he did.

Roaring, he came up out of his crouch. Big Rod and Capper yelled too, startled from a deep sleep, and scrambled up the crater's side. "What the..." yelled Capper.

"Dinner. Over there." Frenz pointed to the gray lump jiggling on the ground not far from them. He cocked another bolt into the crossbow to be safe and walked to the whatever-it-was. "Well," he said, standing over what would be dinner. It was an armadillo-thing. It looked like something had mated with a pill bug, for under the banded gray shell were a dozen or so legs, beefy.

"Ohhhh. Those will make for good eating." Big Rod grinned as he picked up the armadillo. "I'll start a fire."

At last: food.

Big Rod flicked the bone away and wiped his greasy mouth. "Thank the gods!" They sat around a fire on the lip of the crater.

Thank the gods indeed, thought Frenz. *That was close. I don't know how much longer we could have held on.*

"We'll rest until morning; let this settle and then get going. I don't know if we'll find Mutt or Pisser, but we've got to try." *If it was the A-Eye, nothing will be left to find.*

Capper looked around him. "Then what? Where to?"

After a long pause, Frenz stood. "It's always the question, isn't it? 'Where to?' We walk and walk without a destination. If we come across something to eat or trade, it's dumb luck. Something has to change. We've *got* to be more strategic, figure out a smarter way to find food, things to barter, and safety."

He looked at the horizon. "I've never been to one, but up north I heard stories about cities and what could be found in them, things left from The Before, some of it valuable. Even food." He pointed toward the horizon. "The nearest one is up there on the plateau. Getting there would be a tough go and take a while, but it's better than what we've been doing. What do you say?"

Capper nodded. Big Rod grunted.

"All right. Get your gear together, then get some sleep. We'll search for Mutt and Pisser at first light, then head north." Big Rod and Capper stood, each looking toward the far-off City.

And Capper's head exploded, limbs flung akimbo as he hit the ground.

4

At the bottom of the crater, Sophie lay on her back, looking up at the stars or where the stars were. She'd only seen them once or twice, scattered glitter on velvet black. On those occasions when the clouds parted, they always astounded. No wonder her people told tales at night about the stars, about the end of The Before and how the stars were the strewn bits of it all.

Her head rested in clasped hands, elbows spread wide. The day's march had been long, dinner little, and she was tired. Firelight from the dying flames flitted on the crater walls. What would this trek mean for them, her and Markus? The box...what could it be worth? And what was in it? Was that worth anything? Could there be real wealth there, enough to free them from the scavengers' life? Then what? She closed her eyes, thinking, but sleep didn't come until long after the fire had died to a dull crimson.

They woke at first light, drank, ate, and climbed up the side of the crater. In the pale morning light, they could see well enough. Jen pointed north: "This way." Breaths of gray dust dotted the plain as the morning wind picked up on its way to the City. The target of whatever caused the cataclysm, it had once been a great metropolis and a thriving trade center. Now, its skeletal nubs were indeterminate; perhaps it had once been magnificent.

Sophie, groggy from lack of sleep, lagged behind Barth and Jen. Markus lagged still farther.

"We need to pick up the pace," said Jen over her shoulder. "The way won't get any shorter at this rate."

Sophie took her at her word and stepped closer.

"Jen, yesterday when we were talking about Albright, you said you were interested in him. What did you mean? Did you want to have a relationship with him?"

Jen kept walking but slowed, so Sophie walked beside her. "Are you asking if I loved him, or thought I could love him?"

"Uh-huh."

"I told you, Albright was as commanding a man as I'd ever seen. Remember that I was alone with a village growing around me. People expected me to have answers to questions I'd never even thought of. I was young and didn't know if I could live up to their expectations. Then there appeared this man who was so confident, so positive about his way in the world— it took my breath away. I saw in him what I wanted to be, how I wanted to be. His aloofness made him even more attractive. I guess I was falling in love with him. Looking back now, though, I'm not sure if it was because I wanted him or because I needed him. Is that what you wanted to know?"

"Yeah. I want to know how you knew, how you felt, what that feeling was like. Sometimes when I think about Markus…"

"You'll know when you know, Sophie. I hadn't felt that way before and haven't since, so I'm no expert. It's just something you know. I guess it's different for everyone.

"I do know this, though: Whatever I felt, it wasn't enough to close the distance Albright kept between us. I never knew what he wanted, but in the end, it wasn't me. And yes, it hurt and still hurts sometimes. I don't think that's something you ever really get over."

Late in the afternoon, they dropped down into a protective crater.

"Barth, we need meat. Will you see what you can find up there?" Jen nodded at the crater's top. "I'm thankful for the bread, but we need something more. See what you can find, will you?"

Barth picked up his crossbow, trudged up the side

of the crater, looked back at his companions, and disappeared over the top.

Hunting on the plain was always a gamble. Sometimes the game was almost plentiful; other times, there was nothing to be had. If it was there, though, Barth would bring it back to the fire waiting at the bottom of the crater. He could almost smell meat charring over the open flame.

He scanned the horizon from the crater's edge to get his bearings. Finding markers was not easy; the plain looked the same in all directions, pitted and worn. It was a wonder Jen knew her way to the City. Turning, he saw a rough pile of stones left in the past by other travelers. Those would do.

Barth tramped along, watchful, and cocked the bolt in his crossbow, pulling it to him. That sound, the click, brought a wave of memory. It was misting, the sky a dark gray roiling with low clouds. He was very young, outside with his mother and father, and heard it, that click. He turned to see them: men, yelling and waving weapons, coming for his parents.

One of them grabbed Barth's mother. His father, a big man, rose and shouted. The rest of them descended on him, beating him with clubs until he dropped to the ground. His mother wailed, fell, and was splattered in the head by a blow. It was over.

Rushing to his mother, Barth was pushed away by one or another of the men. There was nothing to be done, her glazing eyes unseeing. His father never moved.

Barth shook off the memory, blinking his eyes to erase what he saw as if that would help. He checked the plain for movement or telltale dust drifting in the light wind but saw nothing.

From the day he lost his parents, Barth, like many others, was shuffled from place to place, to a relative or stranger. Always large, people thought he'd be a good worker, strong and obedient, and rarely refused to take him in. Part of that was true: he was strong. But never obedient.

Selena was slim, brown, and feisty. Barth had seen her the first day he'd moved to an "uncle's" mine in the far west scrub hills. Maybe it was her large brown eyes that drew him to her or her laugh, but she was the first girl who'd stirred him. He stopped and stared whenever she was near.

"I'm Barth," he said the first time they were alone behind a shed crammed with scrap from the mine. "You're…?"

"My father said I wasn't to speak to you."

"I'm Barth." He stood straighter.

"I know. My father said you were big and dumb, and I wasn't to speak to you. At all."

"How old are you? I'm seventeen."

"I told you: I'm not to speak to you."

"But you *are* speaking to me." *She's so pretty.*

She blushed, and a small smile escaped her lips.

"You *are* talking to me, and if we keep talking, you'll find out I'm not stupid. Big? Yeah, but not dumb."

Selena looked up at him, those brown eyes wide. "If my father finds out, we'll both be in trouble."

"He won't find out," Barth said as Selena's father rounded the shed, stopping and staring. He was not a big man, but lean and had what his kids called "old man strength."

"Selena, get to the house."

Barth watched her go and could feel the old man seething, eyes burning into his back. He turned. "Sir, I know you told Selena not to talk to me. It was my fault. She was only saying she wouldn't. Talk to me."

Barth wasn't ready for the old man's fist, but he stayed on his feet. "Kid, we don't know who you are or anything about you. You're just a big kid that's got no future, someone my daughter should have nothing to do with. I know your kind; I've seen your kind. You're a dead end. Stay away from Selena, hear me?" he said, shaking his finger at Barth.

He turned on his heel and followed Selena. Barth stood by the shed, rubbing his jaw. The old man had given the punch all he had, but it hadn't amounted to much on Barth's end.

Barth watched Selena's father walk toward the house. That's when it hit him, the vision. In a crowded hallway he saw Selena flounder and fall; stomping feet crushing her as she struggled to get up. The scene was as clear and real as she'd been a moment ago. Barth saw her noiselessly scream, felt her pain, smelled her blood. He saw her die as the scene faded to black.

This was the gift from his great-grandfathers long past. The gift of vision. The curse of vision.

He slumped against the edge of the shed, shaking.

The light was fading fast. Barth had nothing to show for his hunting, had seen nothing. *Another night with no meat?* Then, movement. Something on the side of a crater not twenty meters from him had moved. A rockslide? He stepped to the edge and peered down to see what it was.

It was a man. Swaying.

5

Firelight played on the man's face, his eyes shadowed slits. Jen eyed him through the fire's smoke. Bearded, he looked to be in his forties, but it was hard to say in the poor light. He was dressed in a long-sleeved brown tunic, belted and torn. He wore no shoes.

Since Barth had stumbled out of the darkness with him, the man hadn't spoken. After he'd drunk all the water they could spare, he started on some of the woodland hard bread.

After a while, Jen said, "What's your name?" *He would be a handsome man with some meat on him.*

The man looked up but said nothing and went back to the bread.

"What happened to you? If Barth hadn't found you, you'd be dead in a day or two. Were there others with you?"

He chewed silently, then, "All dead."

"Who? The others with you? All dead?"

"Ummm."

He gnawed at the bread he held in one hand. His only hand.

Lowering the bread, he looked first at Jen and then one by one at the rest. "Yes. The others are all dead, killed by A-Eye. I ran, fell into the crater. All dead."

Jen leaned in. "Who were the others? What were you doing here?"

"We were brothers. And sisters…looking for the power."

Sophie glanced at Markus, who raised an eyebrow.

"I see," said Jen quickly. "And where were you from, your brothers and sisters?"

"Up north. Michiland."

Jen asked again, "What's your name?"

"Is there any more water?" the man said, looking up.

"No, we've given you all we can spare. What's your name?"

"I'm Luther."

After Luther had finished eating and had fallen asleep, Markus, in a hushed voice, said, "Look, we can't take him with us. We won't have enough food and water if we give him a share. The shape he's in, I'm not sure he'd survive the walk anyway."

"So we leave him here to die?" countered Sophie. "We've got to take him with us. Even if we left him provisions, I don't think he could climb out of this hole. You can see how weak he is."

"We've got just enough food and water for the four of us. If we bring him with us, the only way we'd make it to the City is if Barth gets lucky hunting. Do we really want to chance that?"

Jen stood up and said, "Wouldn't any of us expect to be helped if we were in his position? We can ration water and food, and hope Barth is successful hunting. We can't leave him. We won't leave him."

Markus scowled, shook his head, and went off to bed, muttering. Sophie and Jen followed him.

In the end they left at daybreak, bringing Luther with them. After a small breakfast, Barth pulled him up out of the crater to join the others, and they walked out onto the plain. Luther's meal the night before had strengthened him some, and he kept up their pace, although they stopped more often and rested longer. He tired as the day wore on.

"Luther, last night you said you were looking for 'the power.' What did you mean?" Jen asked. Luther walked beside her, doing his best to match her strides but stumbling.

"Where we're from, up north, almost everyone was of the same faith, our parents and their parents before them. There were other kinds of believers too, but they were outliers. Some of them were people who lived in what we called 'the wild.' Like this, only cold, very cold. Life was much harder there. These people believed the A-Eye ended The Before, and they had enormous power that could restore it. It was the secret of a return to paradise.

"One of them claimed he knew the secret, the secret to restoring The Before. They called him a prophet, *The* Prophet. He had answers to their questions and much more. He knew how The Before ended. He said he could change all that, return them to glory."

Jen stopped and faced Luther. "You're saying he knew Hisry, the Hisry of The Before?"

"Yes. He said he'd learned this from the A-Eye, that he'd 'communed' with them—whatever that means—and learned their secrets. He had evidence."

"Evidence?"

"Yes. We all saw it, a small piece of something, metal, shiny, so shiny. He'd hold it up and wave it around, saying it gave him 'power,' the power from the A-Eye. Many believed him, wanted to believe him. I was one of those.

"Soon enough he had a following, at first dozens, then hundreds. People brought him things—food, clothing. He'd hold what he called 'services,' talk about what he knew, show the evidence. He talked about The Before, how wonderful it was, and that it would be that way again. He said he alone could make it so. He called it 'salvation.' He would bring us salvation."

Markus had joined them and asked, "And did he…bring you salvation?"

"We thought so, thought life would get better. Then, after a while, things changed. He began to order us around, treating those closest to him like servants. And he started to abuse some of the women, those he'd attracted to his services. It got bad. Some of the men got jealous and wanted to kill him. It was chaotic, crazy. Finally, a group of us decided to leave and find the power ourselves. We left and headed south. Here we are."

"So you don't know about The Before," said Jen.

"I didn't say that."

A sharp whistle. Barth raised his hand and stood stone still. They all did. First pointing at his eyes with two fingers, he pointed ahead of them, off to the right. Slowly, he raised his crossbow. Sophie squinted but saw nothing until Barth fired his bolt and a piece of the plain erupted.

They all ran to see what it was.

"A bird-thing," said Markus. "Dinner tonight!" He was right. It was sizable, two-headed, four-legged, and scaled. There'd be enough for everyone. Barth picked it up, and they walked on.

It was late afternoon when Jen called a halt at the edge of a deep crater. After foraging for dry grass and scrub roots, they slid down its side to the bottom. Barth struck a fire, gutted and descaled the thing, and roasted it. They shared bread and water and ate.

Full, they sat by the fire. "Luther, the people you traveled with, were you their leader?" Jen asked.

"Yes. There were over thirty of us when we started south, men and women, even a few children. We knew the trip would be hard, but thought life in the wild had toughened us. We were wrong. Not that we weren't tough, but this was a new landscape we knew nothing about. The weather had warmed as we traveled south, and the ice and snow we were used to disappeared. We had to navigate rivers, lakes, swamps, all things new to us. We lost several in those waters, including some of the children.

"But the real danger was us.

"After a time, some of the men began to covet the women. We thought we'd put that behind us since it had caused so many problems, but soon enough there was trouble, fistfights. Some of the women became frightened and came to me for protection. There were three of them, girls really, who were suddenly always by my side. I was not involved with them in the way the men thought, but that made no difference.

"We'd camped by a stream on the edge of a forest. On the second night there, six of the men who had been the most outspoken about the women came to my tent. They pulled me out and dragged me into the woods. Said I'd stolen their women from them, that it was not fair I had three when they had none, and I would be punished.

"They built a fire, a blazing fire. Three of them lashed my arm to a post and drove it into the ground. Then they raked coals and burning wood under my arm and hand." He stopped.

"They cooked my hand and left me this." Luther jerked back his sleeve. His right forearm was a scarred, tight, twisted purple, his hand gone.

"When I came to, most of our group had gone, but the three women, two more, and a handful of men stayed behind. They bound and treated my arm and stayed with me until I was strong enough to walk. There were nine of us. They still wanted me to lead them. I didn't know where we were going, but I knew what we were looking for: A-Eye and their power."

The fire died down, and all but one went to bed. Up on the edge of the crater, Barth took the first shift, one eye on the newcomer and one on everything else. Shortly after midnight, he rousted Markus to take his place and went to bed. Markus stood guard, hunkered against the chill and drowsy from the day's long walk.

When he woke at dawn, Luther was gone…along with most of the bread, much of their water, and the plassik box.

6

Frenz was on his back, the gray sky bearing down on him. He wiped globs of brain and bone out of his eyes and lay there, listening. What had happened? *Oh. Capper.* He sat up and saw Big Rod stretched out a few meters away, still as stone.

"Rod, we've got to get out of here," he whispered. No response. "Rod!"

Big Rod, face down in the dust, raised a hand, but beyond that didn't move.

Frenz brushed a chunk of hair off his leg, patting himself to see if he'd been injured. He was okay. Rolling to his belly, he crawled to Big Rod and shook him.

"What?" Big Rod moaned.

"We've got to get out of here. Right now. Get your stuff."

Big Rod rolled over and sat up, feeling around for his crossbow and water bag.

Frenz helped him up. They lumbered away from Capper's headless body and slid into a sizable crater nearby. At the bottom they lay, still stunned.

Big Rod wiped at the red smear on the side of his face. "Capper. What happened? Who did that?"

"A-Eye. It had to have been A-Eye. What else out here has a weapon that could do that?" Frenz crawled to the top of the crater, peering over the edge. There was no one there, nothing except for Capper.

"We'll stay down here until dusk, then we'll see to Capper. He's not going anywhere."

Big Rod nodded and closed his eyes. Despite the name, he was a shrimp, a bow-legged shrimp. Someone with a keen sense of irony had nicknamed him, and it stuck. At scarcely a meter and a half and scrawny at that, he wasn't much to look at. He was quick, though, and as tough as nails when it came down to it.

Frenz had found him two years ago, alive under a brush pile in the southern scrubland. They didn't need another mouth to feed, but they couldn't leave him to die, so he became the fifth member of Frenz's pack. Big Rod never explained what had happened, but it didn't matter.

Frenz lay there. *If it was A-Eye, we'd have heard them. They're that noisy. If it wasn't A-Eye, who was it? The weapon that did that to Capper... A city gang might have some-*

thing like that, but why would they come out here? For what? Whoever it was could have killed all three of us. Why kill only one? Were we just lucky…except for Capper? Frenz had been on the plain long enough to have a handle on what went on there: the scavengers, the A-Eye, the lack of water and food. Was there more going on than he supposed? Finally, he drifted off to sleep.

At dusk, they awoke and scouted over the edge of the crater. There was nothing to see. They crawled out and walked to Capper's stiffened body lying in the dust. Big Rod grabbed his water bag, bits of the cooked armadillo from Capper's pocket, and a small brown leather pouch that he handed to Frenz. Capper traveled light.

Looking down at Capper, Frenz said, "The only good to come out of this is Capper's water. We're better off because of it—that and his bits of meat." They rolled his headless body into a shallow crater. Four-legged plain scavengers would take care of it.

Night had settled in, but the murky moonlight was enough to see by. Not ideal to be traveling in the near-dark, but safer now than in daylight. Around midnight, Frenz signaled to stop, and they dropped into a crater for the rest of the night. Big Rod passed Frenz some of Capper's meat, and they ate, drank, and tried to sleep.

At dawn they set out again for the City, watching the horizon, looking for movement and listening for the mechanical sounds of the A-Eye—if that's what was hunting them. If hunted they were. While they could see all around them on the plain, the craters—and what might be in them—posed the greatest danger. They had their crossbows and knives, but those were their only weapons. Years ago, on his long walk down from the north, Frenz had acquired his crossbow from a trader. It was expensive. He'd learned how to make his own bolts for it. Wood, hard or large enough to fashion them, was difficult to come by, but at present he was well-stocked. He was careful to retrieve the bolts he used if he could find them. Against an A-Eye's metal body, however, they were worthless. He needed a gun.

Walking all day, they stopped only to drink. Dusk settled, and they sat on the edge of a crater, Frenz facing one way, Big Rod the other. It was safer keeping watch on the plain than from down in a crater. They ate bits of the armadillo-thing and washed it down with Capper's water. Big Rod took the first watch. Frenz lay down, head on his water bag. He was hoping to get some sleep, but Big Rod, uncharacteristically, wanted to talk.

"I heard once about the weapons A-Eye use. They're a part of them, built in. One is an ordinary gun, like from The Before, but it fires a metal ball that explodes on impact. I think that's what got Capper." He was silent for a moment. "They also have something that fires energy pulses—I don't know what they're called—that disintegrate whatever they hit, leave nothing. Don't have a range like their guns, but close, they never miss."

Frenz grunted. He really wanted to sleep.

"Before I joined up with you, I was with a gang that had guns. We'd found them in one of the cities. Also found a case of buddets. Without buddets, a gun's not worth more than a club, you know. Anyway, I saw them used a couple of times when we needed them. Finally ran out of buddets, and they threw the guns away. Probably not smart, but what good were they now?"

Frenz rolled over.

"I'd been with that bunch when you found me. We were running from The Bishop's gang. Bishop was their boss and as mean as a snake. I never knew exactly what his problem was, but there'd been a long-standing feud between us that had been going on since before I joined up. Had something to do with a woman—there was women in both gangs. One of ours had been stolen from Bishop, and he wanted her back.

"With this woman as bait, we suckered them into following a couple of us into a canyon. Our men up on the cliffs pushed rocks on them after we picked at them with crossbows. They finally stopped shooting. We thought they'd used all their buddets, so we rushed down to gut 'em and end it, but they'd tricked us and started firing again. Most of us were killed. I barely got away after it got dark. Didn't have food or water and had lost my crossbow, so I wandered for a while and then lay down to die. If you hadn't found me…well…"

Frenz was snoring, but Big Rod didn't notice.

7

"Of course I didn't tell him about the box," protested Markus, pacing, twisting his hands. "I'm not stupid!"

"I'm not saying you did, Markus, but how did Luther know what it was? It was hidden the whole time he was with us," Sophie insisted. "And why would he take the box? What good would that do him out here?"

"He's smarter than we gave him credit for," Markus said. "Somehow, he figured out it was worth something. I don't know how, but that doesn't matter. We've got to get it back."

They were all standing on the lip of the crater they'd slept in the night before. Luther's footprints led from it into the dry distance.

Hands on her hips, Sophie went on. "And how can we do that with almost no food or water? Even if Barth can hunt something else down, without water, we'll never make it to the foothills. He didn't just leave; he left us to die!"

"It's not that bad—well, not quite that bad," said Jen, arching her back, stiff from the night before. "We've got a bit left in the water bags we were sleeping on. If we're careful, it'll be enough to get us to the foothills; there's water up there. When Luther and I talked yesterday, he was very interested in hearing about Albright. It sounded like he thinks Albright can lead him to the A-Eye. If that's so, then that's where he'll be headed, to the City to find him, same as us."

For the first time since they'd left the woodland, Barth spoke. "He has a head start of at least five hours and has water and food; he won't need to stop to hunt. That's what'll slow us down. If he goes to the City looking for Albright, he'll be there until he finds him. We find Albright, we'll find Luther, and we'll find the box."

Sophie stared open-mouthed at Barth. He'd spoken.

After a few beats, Jen said, "All right then: to the City," and nodded at the way ahead.

The day wore on. The near-empty water bags sloshed as they walked.

"Markus, I don't know how Luther found out about the box, but he knew we had it, and he played us," Sophie said. "He might have taken the box to barter with Albright for information. That's what he wants, to find the A-Eye."

"Maybe," Markus said. "It's still my fault he took the box and the rest of it. I was on watch, and it was my responsibility. I don't know how he got by me."

"Things happen, Markus," said Sophie, reaching to touch his shoulder. "Worrying about it won't change it. If we have to worry, let's worry about how we'll get to the City without enough food or water."

Markus walked on, but slower, lingering well behind. Since the one-handed fanatic had left with the box and water, he'd had a hard time looking the rest of them in the eye. Sophie said it wasn't his fault, but then whose was it?

At noon, the sun was a milky spot in the gray sky. They stopped to drink and catch their breath. The pace had been aggressive, and they were all winded, even Barth.

Barth had spoken! Even Jen was surprised. In the years she'd known him, he'd never said more than a few words at a time or been one for planning anything, even when pressed. Now it was clear he'd been thinking through how to find Luther and the box. *Why?*

Jen walked ahead alone, lost in her thoughts about what lay ahead. She was not as confident of reaching the foothills as she'd led them to believe. The truth was they could run out of water before then. Without water, with what remained of the hard bread and anything Barth could bring to the fire, they'd still last only a few days. Even doing their best to conserve what was left, she still wasn't sure if it would be enough.

How things had changed since Sophie and Markus first arrived in the woodland with the plassik box. Suddenly, Barth was interested in it and its contents. And Luther? He'd upended everything. *I thought I was a good judge of character, but I completely missed the mark. He was nothing if not a liar and a thief.* Then there was Albright. Since Sophie had asked her those questions about him, emotions she'd long buried kept bubbling up, memories of him popping into her consciousness: his face, his voice, his eyes. *How could I have been so blind those years ago? I was in love with him and let him leave without telling him. Would it have made any difference if he'd known? I'll never know, but at least I'd have said how I felt. How foolish of me.*

Markus trudged forward to walk alongside Sophie. "How far is it to the foothills? Can you see them?"

Sophie pointed. "If you squint, they're there, that low brown line on the horizon." She wiped her brow, flinging sweat onto the dry earth. "Jen says there'll be water in the vales where the rain puddles. We'll need to dig to find it, but it'll be there. You know, I've been thinking about Barth. I didn't think he'd paid attention to what Luther told us, and I never thought he'd be thinking about how to find him. Did you?"

"Not really. To me, Barth's always been Jen's bodyguard, nothing else. He's right, though: we'll find him and the box in the City."

In a moment, Sophie said, "When Jen and I were walking yesterday, she talked a little about Albright. She knew him before he moved to the City, but I didn't know what their relationship was or how she felt about him." She glanced at Markus. "I think taking the box to him was only an excuse for this trip. If Albright can open it, we'll find out what it's worth and what's inside, but the real reason we're going is for Jen to see him. From what she told me, I think she's still in love with him. When she first said we should go to the City, I was excited. But now…"

"Look, if Jen thinks we'll make it, then I do too. I've always thought of the City like something out of a fairy tale, not completely real—even though we've been there. Now I just want to get there alive. Do you remember anything about it? I don't remember why we were there or even who we were with. Do you?"

"Not really," said Sophie. "We were how old, six or seven? You were younger, so you wouldn't remember much. We were there with the family we lived with, went where they took us. We were kids, you know, never on our own." *But now we* are *on our own and might come into money or trade goods when we sell the box and whatever's in it. Could that mean we could quit scavenging? Then, do Markus and I go our separate ways? I don't want that...don't think I want that. But what do I want?* She blushed as she thought back to the morning Jen had asked her about "taking precautions." *Is Markus what I want?*

8

Something woke Frenz. Was it the breeze that had arrived during the night? Or Big Rod's wriggling to stay awake? Or the dream of his wife and children?

The dream was always the same. The sky was clear, the day mild. Frenz, his wife, and their two children were by a lake. The kids played at the shoreline, poking sticks at a yellow leaf-boat floating on the water. The girl's little doll lay beside her. Frenz and his wife sat on rough blankets talking, snacking, watching the kids. Glancing up, Frenz saw his wife's face freeze as she looked past him. That was the last thing he saw. When he came to, they were gone, the three of them. He spent that day and the next and the next looking for them.

In the dream, he didn't see the bloody doll by the water's edge or his wife's single shoe. In the dream, they were just gone. They're still gone.

He never forgave himself.

Frenz pinched his eyes and rose to his elbows. It was his shift. He whistled softly and Big Rod turned, nodding. Frenz grabbed his crossbow, and Big Rod ambled off to sleep. Frenz rose, tucked his crossbow under his arm, and looked northward toward the foothills and the City beyond. If the stories he'd heard bore out, better times could be ahead. He hoped so.

Frenz checked the horizon, then pulled out the leather pouch he'd taken from Capper's body, dumping the contents into his moonlit hand: coins from The Before, four red beads, and a piece of green plassik. He bit a coin. *How were these used? And these red beads…why would Capper keep them?*

Frenz picked up the small piece of green plassik and rolled it between his fingers. *Plassik. Wars were fought over it, or the stuff it was made of—that and water. What must it have been like to have so much that men had the luxury of endless fighting? How stupid. How wasteful. Did one side or another's weapons end The Before? Could this green bit really be the cause of it all?* He started to throw the plassik away but dropped it back into the leather pouch. It was worth something, if only to remind him of Capper.

As dawn broke, Frenz shook Big Rod; they gathered their things and moved on. The extra water helped, but the armadillo-thing meat was about to run out. Both kept their eyes on whatever crater lay ahead, hoping to spy something for the night's fire.

Big Rod had never been to a city. His life was endless walking: cold to hot, dry to wet, high to low, but never to a city. Always walking. Frenz's pack was the best bunch he'd been part of. There was little drama and not much infighting. Frenz made good decisions, and so far they'd had enough of the basics to keep them alive. What had happened to Capper wasn't anyone's fault. It had just happened. The A-Eye were like some of the snake-things he'd seen on the plain; you never knew when they'd strike.

I liked Capper; was sorry to see the end of him. Even with his gimp leg, he always carried his weight. And didn't complain. Not like that damn Mutt. And Capper was funny. We needed that. From what Frenz says, cities can be dangerous. It would have been good to have another hand along when we got there. So it goes…

"What you heard about cities, what was it exactly?" asked Big Rod as they zigzagged through the craters. "You said there might be food, water, and things from The Before. What sort of things?"

"I was in Hio, had been traveling from the north after my family… I liked it there and stayed a bit. There was a place, a watering hole where people came to talk, visit. One of the regulars brought beer to sell. He's the one who told me about the cities," said Frenz. "He said he'd lived in the northeast, near the sea. There are cities there, big ones, some with people in them, and he'd been to a couple. He didn't want to say more, but the beer worked on him, so he finally did."

Frenz took a swig of water from his bag. They'd walked long and hard and stopped on the edge of a small crater to finish off their meat and rest before starting out again. It was midafternoon.

"One city he went to was just a pile of rubble. Metal and the hard, shiny ice that never melts was everywhere. The city had been leveled except for one building, something called a B-A-N-K. That's what the sign said. Not much had been disturbed inside. One room, all metal, was broken open, and he found cans with food in them. And water. Someone had stashed supplies. He took as much as he could carry and got out as fast as he could."

Big Rod's mouth watered at the mention of food. They had to find something to eat.

"Another city was small, out in nowhere, near nothing. There weren't many buildings, but in one, in a little room, he found a gun and buddets. In fact, he found several guns and buddets for them all. Said he bartered those for food and a place to stay for almost a year.

"The city ahead could have all those things…or nothing. Don't know what else we'll find, but it's better than just walking, hoping to stumble onto something. There'll be game in the City to hunt too—rats. I'm sure of that."

"Okay then," said Big Rod. "Let's get going." There were a few hours of light left, so they struck out with renewed interest.

The day was beginning to cool, and the shadows deepened. Frenz stopped and threw up a hand.

"Whoa! What's this?" he said, bending to the ground. Big Rod came up behind him.

It was a footprint, a bare footprint. From the direction of the print, it looked like it was headed to the foothills. Frenz looked ahead at the tracks meandering between craters. A meter ahead, other footprints joined it. More people. "They're headed same as us."

Following the footprints, they trudged until the poor light made it impossible to make out the trail. With nothing to eat and no other reason for a fire, they camped on the edge of a crater and waited for daylight. Frenz took the first shift and settled down into a not-too-comfortable squat for the night.

By dawn, the wind had picked up. Grit filled Frenz's mouth and stung his eyes. "Let's get a move on," yelled Frenz over the roar. "The dust is killing me!"

Big Rod had been in worse but didn't care to

bring that up. It was hard enough to talk and hear what was said in the growing gale. Soon he couldn't tell earth from sky as the wind bellowed and howled. Frenz grabbed Big Rod's shoulder and pointed for him to drop in the crater ahead. They slid to the bottom, covering their faces with handfuls of their shirts.

"I've never seen it like this," yelled Frenz, "but it's a little better here. We'll ride it out, see how long this lasts, and get going after it's over."

Big Rod's cough woke Frenz. Shaking off the dust and dirt, he stretched and stood. He could barely make out Big Rod's dust-covered body; it was a dirt log. "Hey, Big Rod. You awake?"

Big Rod kicked out a leg, dust sliding off in rivulets. "Yeah. I thought that would never end. I've sucked up enough dirt to plant a garden." He sat up and spat, choking.

Frenz dug his crossbow and water bag out of the dust and, after taking a deep swig, sidestepped up to the edge of the crater. He peered over the edge and took a long look. Of course, the footprints were long gone.

"Come on," he said. "The City—and people—are ahead."

9

Luther stumbled forward. Between the plassik box and the water bags, the weight wore him out, but what else could he do but carry them? He had to have the water, and the box was surely a prize. They'd had it covered with cloth and never spoke of it directly, but Markus had said something about taking something to the City. Why would they go to the trouble of hiding it unless it was worth something?

The man Jen had mentioned they were on their way to see, Albright, was more than a recluse living in a ruined metropolis. Luther had heard the name in Michiland, heard he knew as much about the end of The Before as any living man. It didn't sound like Jen and her group knew any of this, or if they did, they wouldn't talk about it.

The dirty sun was high and the heat oppressive. Luther's good arm ached from carrying the box. Two water bags and a third bag half-filled with hard bread crossed over his shoulders, slicing into him, keeping him off balance. One foot in front of the other; that's all he could manage. He could see the outline of the foothills ahead.

In Michiland, none of the cities had amounted to much, at least the ones he'd seen. Except for one called d'Toyt, they were small, what was left of them. He'd been to a few, following the Prophet as he "brought salvation" to the people in the wild. *What's this city, the one ahead, like?*

When Jen mentioned "Albright," Luther could hardly keep a straight face. Of all the people who could help make sense of the end of The Before and the A-Eye, it was this man. He had to talk to him and had to get there before Jen, the boy, that brute, and the pretty girl. What to do about them? Since he'd taken their water, maybe they'd die on the plain, and he wouldn't need to resort to anything more physical. Four against one would be interesting, but they hadn't searched him, or they'd have found the gun and buddets. He had enough for the four of them.

The girl. *I hope I won't have to kill her. If she's lucky, she'll make it even with little or no water. You never know, but she looked to be as tough as that bird meat. And a looker.* Luther kept walking, burdened with water, bread, and thoughts of the girl. *I couldn't believe how they ate up that story about leaving Michiland and the fire and my hand. What is it they say, 'Keep a little truth in every lie'? The girl, espe-*

cially, had concern written all over her face. Or was it pity? No matter, I think she likes me.

"Not far now," Luther said to no one. It was true: he was on the edge of the foothills. A gentle upward slope had finally begun, and ahead, the craters were fewer. Higher up, there was even a bit of green where grasses found sips of water. *Odd, the craters are thinning out. You'd think they'd be thicker closer to the City. Poor targeting, or was whoever did this trying to save as much of the place as they could? At least it'll be easier going except for the uphill climb.* For the hundredth time, he adjusted the straps on his shoulders, bending forward under the weight.

That girl. If she makes it this far, I'll need to separate her from the rest of them…if there is even a 'rest.' Thirst might take them, or the A-Eye. Gods damn them. They took my hand and most of the rest of the flock. If Albright can get me to them, I'll deal with them on my own terms, not those of the Prophet. "That would be a blessing, Brother Luther!" Ha! He laughed so hard he nearly choked, the memory of the Prophet screening in his mind. That last day…

As usual, it was cold, the ground snow hard-packed and the walking difficult. The Prophet crunched through the crust, followed by twenty or so of his disciples. Ahead, a village of heathens loomed on the top of a rise. "We'll bring them salvation," said the Prophet over his shoulder. In the few weeks of this "salvation trip," several hundreds of people had heard the Prophet speak and saw the "evidence," held aloft like silver fire. A few had joined his entourage and were now part of the group that entered the village in silence. People came out of their crude houses, some little more than lean-tos, to stare at this parade. Leading it was the Prophet, compelling, larger than life. Tall and dark, he radiated confidence. All eyes were on him.

He stopped in the middle of the village. Raising both hands high, the Prophet yelled out, "Brothers and sisters! We are here, here to bring you good news, to release you from the bondage of The After! Come forward, come close to hear this wonderful news!"

This always worked. They came from their huts, their shelters; the old, the young, and those who worked to provide for them. In a bit, a crowd had encircled the Prophet, those hanging on the edges coming close to hear what he had to say.

"What's this good news?" yelled someone. "Yeah," cried someone else.

"Ah! The good news!" said the Prophet loudly, turning toward the first speaker. "We come from the south. It's very much like this place. Every place is very much like this place. Do you know why? Do you know why you work so hard, why your life—which should be easy—is not? You've seen them, haven't you? The cities, the beautiful cities, where living was so much easier, where the things you work so hard for were easy to come by, things that were taken from you."

As always, there was a grumbling in the throng at this. Even if they'd never been to a city, they had all heard the stories of The Before and knew the fantastic tales of water that came from pipes, automobiles, and ayoplanes. Ayoplanes!

"And why was this life taken? Who took it? Do you know? Do you know who is responsible for this struggle, The After? And more important, can those who took that beautiful life from us return it? Can they return us to The Before, the way it was, the way life was supposed to be?"

This always got a response, and voices rose. If needed, his acolytes would join in to build excitement. People stepped in closer, elders putting their hands to their ears to hear better. "The answer is…yes!" yelled the Prophet.

Gasps. Always gasps.

"You know the A-Eye. If you've been lucky enough, you've seen them and lived to tell the tale. *They* are responsible for The After. They are the ones who ended The Before. They are the ones who hold the secret to bringing us all—ALL—to The Before. Not backward, but forward into the future that was promised to us, to the future that should be ours, that *can* be ours!"

He had them. He always had them. Who could resist the vision of returning to The Before, the better life? No, not returning, but blazing ahead into a new and wonderful future. This was salvation.

As it always was, it was time to bring out the evidence. "Who, you ask, can do this? Who can bring back The Before? I. Only I. I have been with the A-Eye. I've seen their power. I know what they can do!"

There would always be muttering and if no one else asked for it, one of us would yell, "Show us! Show proof! Show us evidence you've been with the A-Eye!" and out would come the evidence, held high to catch what little sunlight there might be. It was always thrilling, even after seeing it so many times: a piece of incredibly shiny metal no larger than a hand.

"This is from A-Eye. Given to *me*. Given to me in friendship and trust. Given as a token of their promise; their promise to *me* of a better future for us all. What they did—and make no mistake, they were the ones that ended The Before—they can *and will* undo. They will give us back our future!"

At this, the crowd always erupted into cheers and applause. The Prophet was going to save them. He would bring them salvation.

It was at this moment Luther saw her standing still on the edge of the cheering, waving crowd. At first, he thought she was just a child, small, delicate. Then he realized she was a woman, more beautiful than he'd ever seen. He couldn't look away. The Prophet had strictly forbidden engaging with "the heathens" beyond what might be required at his services, but the heart wants what the heart wants.

Her name was Isabella.

Two days later, their entourage, including a half-dozen new converts from the village, departed for the next "nest of heathens." With them was Isabella. She and Luther had to be careful when they met, at night and well out of sight of the others. The Prophet was strict and brooked no disobedience. No telling what he might do if he knew about Isabella and Luther. They found out some days later. Maybe he'd known or suspected all along because when they came upon the A-Eye, it was Luther's name he called.

They'd walked long through a snowscape, trees gaunt wiry shapes, rocks and boulders, black pads laid on white. Coming over a steep hill, there they were at the bottom, a pod of not-human things standing together stone still in a group, mud-colored.

The Prophet raised his hand, and his disciples stopped a hundred meters from the A-Eye. Glaring at Luther, he said, "Sharing the opportunity to lead the way to salvation is my most cherished joy, Brother Luther. *You* are chosen to take us to the A-Eye, to learn from them and to feel the righteousness of their strength. That would be a blessing, Brother Luther! For you, for us all!"

Luther glanced at Isabella and, at the Prophet's urging, strode down the hill and walked into their midst. Stepping into a pit of vipers; that's what it was like. From afar, they appeared large. Standing among them, they were huge. While they'd looked human from a distance, up close, it was clear they were not. Their "heads" were truncated nubs encircled by gray tubes that served some sort of sensory function, like eyes. Their arms ended in multi-tooled clusters. Each body (there were eight of them) was covered with what looked like bolts of assorted sizes.

And they stank. Horribly. Luther's stomach lurched. They paid no attention to him. At first. He raised his hand in greeting.

"I…we're here…" That was all he could say. The one nearest turned toward him. A tight green beam shot from a bolt on its shoulder, and Luther's hand burst into blue flame. Clusters of beams shot from the others, striking his brothers and sisters, igniting them with ghastly blue light. They screamed and began to run, the Prophet first among them. Some escaped, but most fell into smoldering heaps, burned by flashes from the A-Eye. Isabella was among those, her small body crumpled in a charcoal heap of bones. All this Luther saw as he sagged to the ground.

Such a blessing.

10

Luther could feel it now, the earth tilting ever so slightly upward: the foothills. The damnable craters were fewer, replaced by rock and boulders gashed from the bombardment of the plateau above. After the endless sameness of the plain, the layered pieces of the plateau danced before his eyes, reds, browns, and yellow, a different geology.

Dropping down at the foot of a large, banded boulder, he tugged the straps of the water bags from his shoulders. They slid to the ground beside the plassik box. Relief! *How far ahead of them am I? A day? Two if they had to stop to hunt? Or maybe they're still back there, dying. At least I hope the girl makes it. Whichever, I've got to plan for the worst, that they all get this far.* He took a long pull from one of the water bags and dug into the bread, thinking.

In the end, he hatched a plan to take care of them. *What shall I call them? 'The soon departed'? No, that's too cruel. How about 'heathens'? Yes. They're just that.* He'd find the perfect spot for an ambush, a shallow spot with water. There, he'd eliminate whoever was left. The girl he'd take with him to the City. *What was her name? Oh, yes: 'Sophie.'* Not wanting to get too far ahead of himself, he resisted imagining the wonderful future he and the girl would share.

Luther looked back down the path through rocks to the plain below. He was on the obvious trail to the City, but to ensure the heathens stayed on it, he salted it with clues. He dropped one of the water bags, empty now after he'd poured water from it into the second bag. Further up the path, he tore off a piece of bread and dropped it to the side of the path. A critter might get it before the heathens came, but maybe not. It was all he had to work with, and he needed to point them in the right direction.

He set his baggage behind a rock and walked ahead, scouting for an ambush spot. After a half hour, he found it: to the left of the path down a gentle incline was what looked like an oasis. Green grass grew at the edge of a moist pit at the bottom of a hollow. There was even a shrub growing there—or was it a young tree? It had been so long since he'd seen a tree that he wasn't sure. With his bare feet, he scuffed a trail leading from the path to the "oasis."

This would lead the heathens to the pit where they'd dig to find water. It was the first such place he'd seen. They wouldn't be able to resist!

Now, where can I hide so I can see them but they can't see me? He walked down the path and turned to look around him. Above the oasis was a line of sizable boulders torn from the plateau. He'd hide between them until the heathens came, then do what he needed to do.

Which is what exactly?

If they all make it this far, I've got buddets for three of them—the old lady, the brute, and that kid. Then I can grab the girl. If she doesn't make it, I'll shoot whoever does. Can't have them in my way.

Luther walked up to the trail and back down to where he'd dropped the box, water, and bread. With effort, he gathered his baggage and marched back up the path to the oasis, trying as best he could to step where he'd stepped before. The ground was hard, and his footprints were few. He'd spent the day setting all this up. It was going to work.

Luther's leg was beginning to cramp, jammed as he was between two massive rocks thrown from the plateau. He sipped at the remaining water bag and gnawed at a piece of bread while he waited for the heathens. If they followed his clues, they could show up in the next few hours, a little before dark, which would work in his favor. He needed some good luck. Since the episode with the A-Eye that had taken his hand, not much had gone his way. He'd lost Isabella, lost his hand, and found himself south in this wretched country.

He checked his revolver once again, spinning the cylinder on his leg to count buddets. Just enough. If it came to a firefight, he'd be the winner. None of the four heathens had mentioned having weapons aside from the brute's crossbow. He'd have that to contend with, but even one-handed, he was a good shot, and a blade would finish any he only wounded. The more pressing problem was what to do with the girl, assuming she made it this far.

Luther had become accustomed to being one-handed, but some things were more difficult because of it. *She looked like she could be a handful. Not sure how easy it will be to force her to come along with me. Tie her up? How exactly will that work? I can't lace my own shoes. If I had shoes…* He settled back down between the big rocks to wait, occasionally glancing at the plassik box beside him.

They lay in the weak shadow of an enormous, striated chunk of the plateau. Jen lay on her side on the ground, head on arm, asleep. Barth sat with his back against the rock, his eyes slits. Sophie and Markus sat in the shade, side by side, hands almost touching. The sun was near to setting.

"We made it," whispered Sophie through crisped lips. They were at the bottom of the foothills.

"Made it? We've still got to find water and something more to eat," answered Markus. "What water's left in the bags isn't enough to get us far. We've got to find more."

"Jen said there'd be water in some of the vales; we'll dig for it." Sophie glanced at her companions. "I guess we're staying here until morning; I don't see us getting far in this condition. At least we made it across the plain. Can I have a sip of water?"

Markus grabbed the water bag at his feet and shook it. It was almost empty. "Here." He nudged out the bag's stopper and handed it to Sophie. She took a short sip and passed it back. "Thanks."

They put their water bags behind them for pillows and lay down. Exhausted, they soon drifted off to sleep.

Jen awoke at dawn. "Barth, Markus, Sophie, time to go," she said, standing over the sleeping three. "There's water ahead. We've got to find it and that won't happen lying here."

Barth stood first, raking his fingers through his long beard and reaching for his crossbow. Markus and

Sophie, as usual, had spent the night huddled together for warmth. They untangled, Sophie glancing embarrassedly at Jen. Markus stood and grabbed the water bag and what was left of the bread. Each took a short swig from one of the bags and passed it on. They were nearly empty.

"As I remember, we've got a day or two before we reach the edge of the plateau, then another day to the outskirts of the City. Getting to the top of the plateau is never easy; we need to find water before then. Keep your eyes open. We're looking for damp depressions; that's where we'll find water and maybe even some game Barth can bring down." Jen tramped off up the faint trail, jabbing her walking stick into the hard earth. The rest followed.

Markus watched Sophie walking, talking to Jen. How had he never noticed—really noticed—her? He'd always thought of her as a sister; after all, they'd grown up and worked together. He knew she was smart. She *always* negotiated a good deal for the things they found to barter, something he'd never been able to do. And she was inquisitive, interested in whatever was ahead and in the people she met. It was she who ensured their scavenging was successful. Now he found her…beautiful. Maybe she wasn't in the way some people talked about someone being "beautiful," but it was more than the way she looked. It was who she was. Who she'd always been.

Ahead, Barth was wary. The boulders could hide

anything and anyone. While there was always the chance something could spring out of a crater, at least the open plain offered a long, clear line of sight. Here, the damnable boulders created a labyrinth. That creep, Luther, could be behind any of them, waiting.

"Damn!" Markus barked, rubbing the ankle he'd hit against the edge of a rock. "That was sharp!" Blood seeped from the cut.

Sophie stepped back to steady Markus as he reached down to wipe a red smear from the wound. "You've got to be more careful, Markus. Let me look. Jen, hold up a minute, will you? I need to look at this."

Markus sat on a nearby rock, dropping his water bag to the ground. Barth came up from behind and eyed the wound. "Nasty."

It *was* nasty, but not deep enough to sever a tendon. Markus rotated his foot. "It's deep, but it didn't slice anything. I'll still be able to walk. I ought to bind it, try to keep it clean." He patted his tunic to find a piece of cloth he could use but found nothing.

Sophie sat beside him and loosened the dark blue sash around her waist. She cut a length of it off with a small knife. On her knees in front of him, she wrapped it tight around the wound. Markus looked down at her as she worked. He could count on her— always count on her. She never hesitated, didn't whine; she got things done. *How have I never seen how special she is?*

"Thanks. Let's get going." Markus rose, slung the water bag over his shoulder, and they continued on into the foothills.

Around a curve, there, in the middle of the path, was a water bag.

11

Jen turned back to Markus and put a finger to her lips: "Shhhhh!" She signaled for them to drop to the ground and fell into a crouch, leaning on her walking stick. The others did the same, heads turning this way and that.

In a low voice, Jen said, "This is one of our water bags, one that Luther stole. He came this way, just don't know how long ago. Listen."

All they heard was the faint whispering of wind in the grass growing along the path. In a moment, Jen rose. Still softly, she said, "He's on this path, all right. I'm guessing the bag is empty, but Markus, grab it; we may need it later. Barth, here, by my side. We don't know how far ahead he might be." Barth stepped past Markus and Sophie and stood by Jen, intent. "Step out in front of us. We'll follow behind you. And be careful."

They hadn't talked about what they'd do if they caught Luther. Could Barth overpower him? Surely he could, but what if Luther was quick with a knife, or worse, had a firearm? Luther was on this path; finding him was only a matter of time. Then what?

Barth stepped to the front as lightly as a big man could. Trouble was ahead, but how much of it, he wasn't sure. No vision had come to him of what the inevitable encounter would bring. He had learned long ago he had no control over the visions, couldn't conjure them at will. They came to him unbidden, sometimes the meaning almost clear, other times cloudy, like bad water. With no frame of reference, he had to figure out what they meant and who was involved.

The vision about the box he'd had in the woodland had startled him. As Jen had turned it over in her hands, he saw a dark room lit by a strange candle. In it, a man bent over the box. The man straightened, turned, and in his hands was a book. No, thinner than that. The man spoke to someone in a corner, someone Barth couldn't see clearly. As always, there was no sound. They were both agitated. The man waved the thin book up and down, pointing to it again and again. The vision had faded.

It had to be important, what was in the box. But what was it, and why? *All I know is that it has to get to the City. Has to.*

"Come on, Markus. Keep up!" Jen urged. Once again he'd fallen behind, watching Sophie's braided hair swing with each step she took, her body moving gracefully as she marched up the path. He'd watched her since he was young, but now she held his interest in a new way. Was this the same Sophie he'd always known, the girl he'd played and worked with in the pits? Had she changed, or had he?

"He could be long gone and threw this away, figuring it was no longer useful," said Markus, holding the empty water bag.

"Could be," said Jen, glaring at Markus. "Or he could be just ahead. Regardless, we need to be quiet."

The path wound through the rocks, gaining elevation the smallest bit as they walked. "Look! Here's some of our bread." Sophie reached down, picked up the small piece, turned it this way and that, blew on it, and popped it into her mouth. "He's ahead." More wary now, they slowed their pace.

"Jen, when we get to the City, how do we find Albright?" asked Sophie quietly. "Will he be easy to find?

"I don't think that's a problem," answered Jen. "He has a compound at the Hilto and surveillance set up around the perimeter. He'll know we're coming long before we arrive. At least that's what I've been told. He's smart. Not to worry. He'll find us."

Ahead on the rising path, Barth threw up a hand and stopped.

"Barth? What?" whispered Jen as she walked up beside him. Barth pointed down to the left side of the path and made a drinking motion.

"Has he found water? Thank god," said Sophie as she stepped to Jen's side. Below, to the left, was a green swale. Water!

"We'll have to dig for it, but yes, water," said Jen. She gave Barth her hand and together they side-stepped from the path toward the wet below. "Look, Markus. He was here," said Sophie, pointing at a scuffed trail. "Luther was here."

The four of them stepped to the bottom of the swale, to the green wet spot at the bottom. "This is where we need to dig," said Jen. "Find something, a stick, and dig a hole. It'll fill up with seepage. May take a while, but we'll get water. Markus, bring the water bags."

From above, in the shadows between the boulders, Luther watched as Barth and Markus found short sticks and began digging in the wet soil. Soon they had a round, wide, shallow pit. Jen and Sophie sat on rocks, watching it slowly fill with muddy water.

I'll let them do the work for me. Save me the trouble. Luther rubbed the stump of his right arm. *There's time enough.* He sat back deeper into the shadows as water seeped into the hole.

Slowly it leaked into the pit, soon with enough to begin filling a bag. Luther stepped from between the boulders, holding the gun in front of him, pointing at those gathered below around the water hole.

Sophie glanced up, eyes growing wide, her mouth forming an O. Her hands fell to her sides.

Markus and Jen followed her gaze. "Barth," said Jen, nudging him to turn around.

"Well, hello," said Luther, grinning. "You made it. You *all* made it. Congratulations!" he said, marching down toward them. "I'd hoped it would be so. Well... not really."

"Luther," said Jen. "What do you want?"

"For one thing, water when you get it. Barth, fill those water bags."

Barth took one of the bags and stuck an end into the water, holding so it began to fill. Luther kept grinning, wider when he looked at Sophie. She shifted uncomfortably.

"You," he said, tipping the gun at Markus, "use Sophie's belt. Tie her hands behind her."

"We could have died, Luther. Why would you leave us, take our water and food? I thought you were a godly man. Was all that talk about the Prophet lies?" said Jen.

"No. And yes," smirked Luther. "I was a part of the Prophet's following, but all I learned from him was to look after myself first. A little of that story was true, but in the end, it was mostly rubbish. I had no intention of staying with your little group. I've got bigger plans." He pointed the gun at Sophie. "Come here. Sit."

Hands tied, Sophie walked over to Luther, sitting down in front of him, glaring.

"You," he said, again motioning to Markus. "Up there. Get the box and bring it here." Markus did as he was told. "Now tie up Jen. Use her belt. Tie 'er up good and tight, hands behind her." Markus slid Jen's belt from her waist, then held her hands behind her and knotted them tight.

"And now, big man—Barth—tie up Markus with your belt. I want to see him tied up good."

Barth undid his belt, pulled Markus's hands behind him, and tied them tight, the belt trailing to the ground. "Now throw me that full water bag." It landed at his feet with a gurgle.

"Why, Luther? What have we done to you other than show you kindness and share our food and water? Why do this? What will this accomplish?" asked Jen, as she fidgeted behind her back with the knots.

"Well. I've decided to do you all a favor—since you *were* good to me—and not kill you. My little family! On the other hand, I can't have you following me, so…" The gun jumped.

Sophie screamed. Jen gasped, hand to her mouth. Markus stared in shock. Barth fell to the ground, grabbing his left leg above the knee. Blood spurted through his fingers.

"You. You're coming with me." Luther looped the water bags and bread over Sophie's shoulders. He tucked the gun into his belt, worked the box up under his ruined arm, grabbed Sophie by her hair, and yanked her up. "This way."

Markus watched in horror as they climbed up the trail to the path to the City. *No!*

THE CITY

12

A million people. Give or take. Ken Baker was proud of that number. His hometown was truly a metropolis, the largest west of the Mississippi or what had been the Mississippi. That river had long since dried up along with most of the inland waterways. The City sat on a high plateau below a low winter-snow mountain range that had blessed it with water—remarkable and a godsend. That, and a prime location, had nurtured a booming economy. At its founding, no one thought the City would ever be more than a convenient stop on the way west (or east). Time and water changed that.

Lazy avenues lined with soaring trees meandered through the City. Verdant parks dotted the cityscape. Families spread blankets and ate from baskets while children ran laughing. It was a city built with care.

Early evening was Ken's favorite time of day. Waning sunlight caught the tops of buildings, leaving the streets below in deep canyons of shade. He sat at a small, round table in front of his favorite café, legs crossed, hand on a white coffee cup. Yes, he had errands, places to go, things to do, but those could wait. *How lucky I am to live here, to be a part of all this. If I could, I'd stay here all day, every day.* He finished the coffee, stood, dropped a tip on the table, and walked into the coming night. That was the moment the first bombs hit.

Stubbled shadows seeped across the tile floor. It was cracked, some tiles missing. Not in terrible shape, really, after three hundred years or so. The building had been a Hilto hotel. At least that's what the stone letters out front said.

In the courtyard, those tiles, pounded by the feet of the terrorized after the bombs started to drop, gave way to silence and the slow drift of ash. Occasional footprints of a healthy few marked the tiles, but those, too, finally disappeared. The numbing drought that baked the plateau continued unabated. The City roasted, water long gone from the mountains. Year after year, dust settled on the tiles and drifted into dunes to cover them. Blood-red sunsets bespoke the clogged and dead sky as the global heat dome dried everything up. For generations.

Finally, a patch of blue.

Slowly the sky cleared. The heat dome and what had created it dissipated, and the air cooled. Those first blessed drops of rain fell on parched soil, washing the tiles clean at last. Seeds found footholds, and the first green things bravely stood in the City. Finally, the mountains began leaking water onto the plateau through long-dried riverbeds. Over decades, scrubs and then trees emerged and grew. Some towered over the remains of crumbled buildings while some grew up through them, supporting leaning walls. Through all this, the tiles of the Hilto remained.

Finally came people, descendants of the few who had survived those centuries ago. They'd lived in the City's underground tunnels and warrens, subsisting on caches of canned and dried food and fungi grown in the near-dark. In cisterns long forgotten, they found water. At the greening of the City, enough of them came up to the blue sky and rubble to rebuild shelters among the fallen skyscrapers. They were home at last.

"I told you. I told you," Kendella's mother ragged. "Don't keep a lid on it, and you know what will happen!" They sat across from each other at a rough wooden table. The room was quiet, a light breeze blew through the open side, and sunlight slanted through trees to dapple the floor.

Kendella Baker rolled her eyes. "Mom, she's grown. She's going to do what she's going to do. Not much I can do about it. It's not like you've had the 'mothering thing' all worked out. And I turned out okay, wouldn't you say?"

This always got her mother. Kendella had been as wild as Ruby, wilder in fact, and her mom, Doritz, had let her run free. Yes, she'd gotten into trouble, but was there a kid growing up in the City who hadn't?

"I just don't know why you can't rein her in a bit," said Doritz, pushing back her unruly gray hair. "That bunch she's running with is trouble, all of them. You know she'll get pregnant…just like you did. You ready for that? You ready to be a grandmother?"

No, Kendella wasn't ready for that. "Grandmother" didn't fit into the future she imagined. In the back of her mind, she had her heart set on finding a man—or even a woman—to partner with. How much easier it would be with someone at her side. She was about forty, tall and toned, with short, dirty blond hair and the most beautiful eyes in the City. At least that's what her last boyfriend had told her. And she could work as hard as any man. Her job was important and, by extension, so was she. No, she wasn't ready to be a grandmother. Ruby would need to be careful so she didn't end up like Kendella, pregnant at seventeen with no partner and no prospects. She was called "K," just "K."

After Ruby had come along, Kendella had to figure out how to provide for herself and Ruby. She'd lived with Doritz for a while until she found work that allowed her to move into a place of her own, but she'd needed more. She was eighteen and had a baby.

Kendella had heard of it, the Library, deep beneath the City in what had been a vault for some kind of business, a bank maybe. In it were paper books, countless numbers of them, that held the wisdom of the past. No one knew exactly where the Library was, at the end of what labyrinth beneath what building. If she could find it, she'd find *how things worked*, the details of The Before that were lost and forgotten. If she could find something there that would bring the past, even a small bit of it, back into the world, it would give her stability and Ruby a future. Her life would be on a different trajectory.

She stood in front of one of the buildings that had escaped the worst of the long-ago bombing but had softened and settled over the years. Louis The Drunk told her he'd found a pit with no bottom in this one, but standing in front of it now offered her little hope. What had been the entrance was only a hole, a clearer place amidst the debris. She picked her way over masonry and around broken concrete pylons that had once supported floors above. She wasn't concerned about going up. It was down, and what she might find, that interested her. This might be the way to the Library. Or not. Reaching into her bag, Kendella took out a candle and firestarter and pushed deeper into the rubble.

13

If he'd known she'd be so stubborn, Luther would have reconsidered kidnapping the girl. Not kidnapping, really, just facilitating her deliverance from the hands of the heathens. It was a favor he was doing her. Why she wasn't grateful, he couldn't understand. He'd given her bread, water, and some of whatever it was he'd found on the side of the trail (yes, it smelled none too good, but meat's meat). Still, she squirmed and resisted him through the foothills. He had the bruises and scrapes to show for it.

"We'll be there tomorrow. Can't you just settle down a bit?"

"If you'd loosen this, I might," she said, holding up her bound wrists. Luther had retied them in front of her so she could carry the box. "And you can carry this yourself!" She threw it at him and sat down.

"I'll say it again. If I'd left you with the others, you'd be dead by now. The brute's injury will either kill him or drag them all down with him. Can't you see I've done you a favor? Why can't you be a little more appreciative?"

Sophie frowned. "Why do you want me, Luther? What do you think? That I'll fall in love with you? Want you? That we'll be lovers, partners? That's the last thing that could ever happen!" She looked at the gun always tucked into his belt.

Well, this hasn't turned out as I'd hoped, thought Luther. *What can I do with her? Use her for barter? Albright might take her in exchange for information about the A-Eye. If I can find him.* "Get up, Sophie. We've still got a way to go."

Sophie begrudgingly got to her feet, took one last look back at the empty plain below, and stumbled in front of Luther. He pushed her with the box he held under his good arm, the one with the gun at the end of it. Sophie had a remaining water bag and another bag for bread slung around her shoulders. Walking was difficult on the uneven ground, the path forward to the City littered with rock.

"You know, Sophie, when we get to the City, I'll have options. I'm sure you understand that. If I were you, I'd be thinking about how my behavior affects my future."

Sophie ignored him. On the trek through the

foothills, she'd watched Luther's every move. Shouldn't it be easy to disarm and overcome a one-armed man? Apparently not. Luther was attentive, suspicious, and meticulous when dealing with her. She never saw an opportunity to escape, much less over-power him and get his gun. Until she could do that, all she could do was wait.

And what about Jen, Markus, and Barth? Poor Barth! Luther wasn't just ruthless, he was cruel. They'd have to make it to the City to find help for Barth, but could they even make it there? His leg looked horrible, and he was in such pain. *I don't know who's in the worse predicament.*

Big Rod's mouth hung open as he looked down at the scene below. Yes, there was a small pool of water, but the last thing he expected to find was other people, much less three of them. Frenz stood beside him. "Well, look at that," he said. Around a watery depres-sion lay a small woman, a young man, and a giant. The giant was clearly in distress. His leg was propped up and bandaged, a brown strip of cloth wrapped tightly around the thigh as a tourniquet.

The woman spoke: "Help us. Can you help us, please?" Big Rod lowered his crossbow.

"We need help getting him up to the trail," the

woman said, pointing at the giant. "We can't do it by ourselves."

Frenz lowered his bow and walked down to the green swale, followed by Big Rod. "What's happened here?" he asked as they approached the three. On the ground lay three cloth belts. They'd managed to untie each other.

"We were ambushed." For the first time, the young man spoke. "Barth got shot in the leg. The buddet passed through, but he still can't put much weight on it. Can you help us get him up to the trail?"

"We can do that," said Frenz. "Have all your things? You," pointing at Markus, "what's your name?"

"Markus. I'm Markus. That's Jen, and this is Barth."

"Markus, help me with him; you on one side, me on the other, and we'll walk him up. Ready?"

Barth nodded.

Frenz and Markus each got on a side, threw one of Barth's arms over a shoulder, and stood. Barth grunted, rising on his good leg. Together, the three of them hobbled up to the path to the City. Jen and Big Rod followed with full water bags, crossbows, and the rest.

When they reached the trail, they sat Barth on a large, flat rock. His leg had begun to seep, but he said nothing.

Turning to Jen, Frenz said, "So tell me, how did this happen? Who did this?"

"It'll take a minute to tell. Let's move up there where it's more comfortable," she said, pointing to a wide space where they could all sit. There she told the story of how they'd found Luther, who he was, how he'd stolen the box, kidnapped Sophie, and taken their food and water. As she spoke, Frenz pulled out his medpack and began cleaning Barth's wound, applying a disinfectant powder.

"We saw your footprints and I guess his too," said Big Rod after a sip of water. "Wondered if we'd catch up with you, who you were. Think this guy, Luther, is headed to the City?"

"We know he is. That's where he'll find what he's looking for, the A-Eye," Jen said.

"An idiot!" laughed Frenz. "Who in their right mind would intentionally want to find the A-Eye? He deserves whatever he finds!"

"Agreed," said Jen, "but we've got to find him, and the box, and Sophie. God knows what he'll do to her."

"Or her to him," interjected Markus, smiling. "Frankly, I'd hate to be in his shoes."

"You say you were on your way to the City before all this happened, right? Might I ask why?" said Frenz.

Jen looked at Markus first, then said, "The box

that Markus and Sophie found is valuable—or we think it is—since it's large and made of plassik. In the City there's someone who can tell us what it's worth. And what's inside it that could also be worth something, but we can't open it. We think Luther's going there too."

14

Through the rubble at the back of the ruined building, Kendella had found a hole that led her down to the Library. By the time she stood in its center, she was exhausted and filthy, holding a lit candle high. All around her were books. Unlike many of the Loca—that's what the folk of the City called themselves—she'd learned to read, taught by those who could. These Loca were the City's elite and held it together. A loose group of about twenty, they made the decisions that kept the City alive, kept it working for everyone. It was they who decided where to locate the gardens and animals for the City's food sources. They ran schools for youngsters, and it was they who provided health care, especially for the elderly. These were the people Kendella aspired to be. She wanted a place at their table. Impress them, and they'd hold a chair for her, pull it out, and, as she sat, ask if she wanted a cool drink. What would it take to get that kind of attention?

What would that be, the thing she needed, the skill that would set a course for her? That's what she was looking for in the Library, something that would pay enough to provide for Ruby and give her status. Something to set her apart...and above. She'd seen the scorn heaped on Doritz—an unwed mother—and then followed right in her footsteps. Kendella was determined to break that cycle.

Revered as valuable possessions from The Before, a few books were scattered in homes around the City. Doritz had one. All the magical things Kendella read about in them happened because of "power." It made The Before run, made everything run. Called "electricity" and "energy," it ran through "wires" and in and out of walls. It was everywhere the people of The Before wanted it to be.

If Kendella could discover this power, could she turn it into the living she needed to provide for Ruby? More than that, could it elevate her status, give her the attention she sought, and lift her from the life that Doritz had? Surely there were books about it in the Library.

Kendella knew the Library held two kinds of books: Truth and Lies. What she needed was the truth about this power, about how to make it. She'd find this in the Truth section. On that first day she found nothing, but she came back the next day with more candles, water, and food. Every day she visited the Library. Gradually she narrowed her search: energy production and conservation, then hydraulic engineering, and finally generation of electric power. After days of looking, she found what she needed: "Hydroelectric Systems: Installation, Operation, Management, and Repair."

The day Kendella left the Library, she knew she would find a place at the table and stay there. Her life growing up with Doritz had not been easy, but with time and perseverance, she could change that for Ruby, a toddler. With a stub of a candle, she found her way back up through the rubble and stepped out into the sunlight holding a book, her ticket to the future.

As a child, Kendella had played along the banks of a river that came down from the mountains above the plateau. It started there, but where it ended no one knew. All its branches disappeared into the earth at one place or another along their courses. Where the water went from there remained a mystery. It was this river that had brought the City back to life so long ago. At first, it kept the thirsty Loca alive. Then it helped the new gardens and small farms flourish and kept livestock—the rabbits and fowl—alive. This was the river that could drive the turbines for hydroelectric power. It had done so before. Kendella's challenge would be to create—or find—the equipment that would turn rushing water into power.

Louis the Drunk had been right about the Library. Did he know where there were generators for the hydroelectric power plant, whatever bits might be left from The Before? Kendella reasoned they had to be along the river, but where? She knew its tributaries on the edge of the City. Where she hadn't ventured was in the heart of the City itself. She went to see Louis.

He'd come by his name the usual way: he was always drunk. They said that as a young man, he'd discovered the secret to brewing and got lost in his wares. Over the years, he'd only become more alienated, withdrawn, and mean. He was shunned and rarely seen in daylight. Rumors placed him in the twilight voids in the City, the cavernous underground vaults and small warrens. He knew the City's underbelly.

Louis's lean-to on the north edge of the City was most unpleasant and always avoided. That's where Kendella found herself standing in front of a softened pile of rubble.

"Louis?" she called, leaning down into the opening to his lair. "Louis, are you there?" It was midday and nothing stirred. "Louis!" she shouted louder.

"What?"

"Louis, I need to talk to you. It's K. Please come

out." *If I have to go in there, I'll suffocate.* She held a cloth over her nose.

"Who is it?"

"It's K. Please. Come out." She stood back from the entry to his den, back into the sunlight and fresher air.

After a bit, Louis the Drunk's head appeared. He rubbed his eyes and squinted. "What do you want? It's early."

"Louis, I need to talk to you about something important. Please come out."

The head disappeared. In a moment it reappeared, followed by a body, squat and leathery. Louis was clothed in an assortment of ragged clothes he clutched to himself. His stringy beard and unkempt hair were the color of his unshod feet.

"What? What you want to talk about?"

"Louis, I found the Library. You were right. It was there. Thank you."

Louis shrugged. "What of it?"

"I need your help with something else, something you might know about. Something important." Kendella had brought the book from the Library. She opened it and stood as close to Louis as she could stand. "Have you seen anything like this, or any part of something like this?"

Louis took the book in his dirty hands and brought it closer to his face. "What is this? What are these?" he said, pointing to the machinery in a diagram.

"This is a power plant driven by water…to produce electricity. It's from The Before, and I believe it, or parts of it, may still be here…in the City center. Have you ever seen anything like this? It would be near water."

Louis looked long and hard at the diagram, then turned the page over to a photograph of a turbine and generator. After a minute, he said, "Yes. I've seen these. Big, very big. Many of them. Under the dam. I can show you."

15

"What is that? Is the City on fire?" asked Markus. In the distance, light splattered against the nubs of buildings and shone through the trees on the outskirts of the City. Jen, Markus, Barth, Frenz, and Big Rod stood awestruck.

"It's not fire… It's…I don't know," said Jen.

"Is it from the A-Eye?" asked Big Rod uneasily.

Clouds lay low over the City, reflecting pale, splotched light. It was like nothing they'd ever seen.

"I'm not going there tonight, that's for sure," said Big Rod. "No way. Maybe in daylight, but not tonight until we know what that is."

"We wouldn't be able to find anything tonight anyway, so yeah, let's camp here, and tomorrow we'll move into the City," Frenz said.

Markus glanced at Jen for confirmation, but she

didn't respond. Since Frenz and Big Rod had found the travelers at the bottom of the swale and they'd resumed their trek, Jen had said little. Barth's injury had affected her deeply, and Frenz had become the group's de facto leader. He'd gotten them to the outskirts of the City.

"There," said Frenz, pointing at one of the now-infrequent bomb craters. "We'll camp down there for the night. I don't know if A-Eye are in the area, but it'll be safer. Barth, you should stay up here. It'll be easier on your leg than trying to walk down and back up. That okay with you?"

Barth nodded. Even with the slow-going, his leg had given him fits, still weeping from the gunshot wound.

"I'll stay with him," said Markus. "Just in case."

Markus helped the big man to the ground, laid him back on his water bag, then sat beside him. He needed quiet and time to think. Since Sophie had been marched off by Luther, Markus had been trying to make sense of it, how he felt. The jumble of emotions confused him, but this he did know: he was worried for her.

After collecting firewood (wood!) and borrowing Barth's firestarter, they built a fire at the bottom of the crater. Big Rod took his crossbow and hoped to find something to cook but returned empty-handed. There was a bit of the hard bread left, which they shared.

The three sat by the fire. "You said there was a box that Luther stole. Why do you think it's valuable?" asked Frenz.

Jen poked the fire, sending cinders into the sky. "It's plassik for one thing. Hard to find at this size. For another, there's something in it. We couldn't open it in the village, but I'm sure Albright can."

"Who is Albright? How do you know him?"

"I knew him from before, in the village. We were…friends. He's smart, and if anyone can open the box it'll be him. And whatever is inside, he'll know what to do with it." She stabbed the fire again. "And you, Frenz. Why were you going to the City?"

"Tired, I guess. Tired of walking, scavenging. Thought it might be better in the City. I don't know. Doesn't matter. That's where we're going."

Big Rod nodded.

Frenz continued, "And what about the girl? Who is she? Why did Luther kidnap her, Jen?"

"Her name is Sophie. I've known her since she and Markus were kids. They grew up together." Jen glanced up at the crater's ridge where Markus sat, lit by firelight against the dark clouds. "I think she and Markus…well, I don't know, but something's going on between them. She's a pretty girl, smart and tough, tougher than she thinks. Luther was taking a shine to her, wanted her for the usual reasons, I'm afraid. She'll be a handful!"

"Any idea where he could be taking her in the City or why?"

"Luther's looking for Albright just like we are, but for different reasons. He has this insane idea that through the A-Eye, he can restore the world…yes, the world…to the way it was in The Before. Albright is an expert on Hisry and knows all there is to know about the A-Eye. Luther thinks Albright will help him." She glanced again at the crater's rim. "We think he's crazy, but now that he has Sophie, we've got to take him seriously. It worries me."

"Sounds like it should," whispered Frenz.

"How did you get so screwed up?" asked Sophie. "What happened to you?"

Luther curled his lip and shrugged slightly. "You haven't been through what I've been through. You couldn't know." He shook his empty sleeve.

"Oh. That. That's what's made you the mess you are?" spat Sophie. "You think you're the only person who's had it tough? Did you have parents? I never knew mine. Have you had to scramble for every meal? I have. *Every* meal. What makes you so special that you think you can lie and steal from us and then save the world through some stupid agreement with the A-Eye? You're an idiot."

Sophie was bound, hand and foot, sitting and

lashed to a tree on the far edge of the City. The plassik box lay at her feet. She could barely move. Her gray shift was torn and filthy. Too much of her leg showed, earning Luther's stare. She saw him looking at her.

"I swear, if you touch me, I'll kill you. I will."

Luther spun his revolver's cylinder against his leg. "Was I not clear, Sophie? Your future is completely in my hands—what *I* choose to do with you. Behave and things could go well. Continue to defy me and you'll end up like your big friend, Barth…or worse. Your choice."

Sophie sulked. He was right. There was not much she could do other than to do what he said. If he did touch her, though—it didn't matter the consequences —she'd kill him or die trying. "All right. Now what, Luther? You don't have the faintest idea of where Albright is, do you? Or any idea of how to find him. What's the plan, big man? Or should I call you 'stumpy'?"

Luther rose quickly and backhanded her. "Wait here," he said, picking up a water bag. "And don't go anywhere!" He laughed as he strode off.

Kendella pushed away from her desk, chair scraping the floor. She wore a light tan rabbit-cloth jumper almost the color of her hair, a sign of her station.

Rubbing her eyes, she took a drink of water, clear and cold. All day, nearly every day, she was in this office watching the gauges. This was her job: running the hydroelectric power plant that provided electricity to those parts of the City that could get and use it. At night, it powered lights in the City center, keeping predators at bay and the City safer for nighttime travel. Her job brought her the respect she'd sought and enough pay—mostly in kind—to keep her and Ruby alive…and more.

"Louis, I'm going home. Stay until the lights fire at dark, then lock up, will you?"

Louis, no longer The Drunk, nodded. "Okay. See you tomorrow." He rubbed his clean-shaved chin. "I've got it covered."

Kendella grabbed her jacket and walked up the stairs to ground level, shaking her head. *Talk about a change of character.* Louis, somehow, had found in the power plant something to live for, to stay sober for, and now he was second in command. He'd earned Kendella's trust.

On the path, she shrugged on her gray jacket, then stood for a moment, eyeing the sky. This was her favorite time of day. Birds chirped on the way to their nests, and the light softened to burnish the nubs of the buildings. If there was a breeze, it was always sweet from cookfires around the City. She set out for home, but from the corner of her eye she saw movement in the surrounding greenery. Kendella stood still, her hand clutching the knife on her belt. It was a shape in the shadows. She slowly turned toward it, gripping the knife harder. Out of the shadows walked a man, thin, barefoot, one-handed.

"Hello," he said.

16

Kendella stared, mouth open. *Who is this?*

"Hello. I'm Luther."

"I'm K, Kendella." She continued staring. "You're not a Loca."

"Loca?"

"The people, the people who live here. The Loca."

"No. I'm not from here. I came from the plain. We walked here."

Kendella stared in disbelief. "Across the plain? You walked here?"

"Yes. Me and my companions."

"And where are they, your companions?" She glanced behind him and saw only the dark forest.

"Dead. Or almost all dead. Do you have any water?"

Kendella shook herself. He didn't look threatening. In fact, he was barely standing. "Sure. You're thirsty. Give me your water bag, and I'll get you water."

She trotted back into the power plant and returned with a near-full bag of water, cold and clean. As Luther stepped closer, she handed it to him, saw he took it with only one hand. Up close, she could see how the walk had ravaged him. His cheekbones bit through the skin on his face; his gray eyes had sunk into his head. He drank from the bag thirstily.

"Luther, you said *almost* all your companions were dead. Are some alive? Where are they?"

Water ran down Luther's chest, staining his tunic as he gulped it. "Back there," he said, pointing over his shoulder with his stump.

"Do you want to bring them here? Do you need help to do that, Luther?"

"No, they're too weak right now. I'll take them this water, and that will help. Do you have any food?"

"No, not with me. I can get some bread, though. I think the bakery is still open."

"Maybe tomorrow. Right now, it's the water we need." He continued to guzzle from the water bag.

"I can do that for you. What else do you need?"

Luther blinked. "We're looking for a man named Albright. Do you know him?"

"Of course. I mean, yes, I know him. After you've drunk, I can take you to him or bring him to you."

Luther scowled, pursing his lips. "No! I have some

things to take care of first, then I'll see Albright. Where can I find you tomorrow?"

"See that door there?" She pointed at the stone building she'd just left.

Luther nodded.

"I'm there every day. From dawn to dusk. Go inside and shout my name—they call me K—and I'll come."

"All right then. Tomorrow, K, and thank you for the water." Luther turned and disappeared into the greenery, leaves folding in behind him.

Dawn broke early on the edge of the City. To the north, the mountain snow blazed pink and white as the sun slipped over the horizon. Barth had had a fitful night tossing and turning as his leg burned with new infection. Markus had slept no better, worrying about Sophie. God, he hated Luther. *When we find him…*

"Hey," shouted Frenz up to the crater's lip. "Breakfast? I can bring you something."

"That would be great," Markus called back.

Frenz sidestepped up to the lip of the crater, followed by Big Rod and Jen. After handing Barth and Markus the near-last of the bread and a water bag, they all sat and ate.

"So, what's the plan?" asked Big Rod, mouth full.

"How do we find Albright and get Barth's leg looked at? He's not doing so good." He addressed the questions to Jen.

"Albright knows we're here. I'm sure of it. We could wait for him to come to us, or send someone to bring him to us, but Barth needs tending to sooner than that. We need to get him to the City center and find help. Let's get our things together and get to it."

After finishing breakfast and pulling their gear up from the crater, they set off. Big Rod was still wary about what they'd find in the City. Last night's strange lights had spooked him. Jen took the lead since she knew the way. Although it had been years since she'd been to the City, the main paths had not changed, and she could lead them into the City. Markus and Big Rod struggled to help Barth. The big man was a handful.

Frenz caught up to Jen and asked, "You've been to the City before, yes? How long ago?"

"It's been years, but yes, I've been here three times. Once as a child, and then again before I founded the village. The last time was after Albright moved here. I was looking for him. Never found him, though."

"Jen, you said you knew Albright from before. How? Did he live in your village?"

"No, he never actually lived *in* the village—said he didn't feel comfortable there. Most people thought of him as one of us, though. He never said where he'd been before, just somewhere out west. He was a private person."

"How did he end up in the City?"

"He thought he was on the verge of finding out what ended The Before. That was his passion, Hisry. He was determined to find that out. When he left, he said he'd find the answers he needed in the City. We…I…hated to see him go."

"So, you were more than friends?"

"I was young," was all Jen said.

A glorious water-splashed plaza shaded by tall eucalyptus trees had long ago been in the middle of the City, a once-beautiful stone fountain at its center. The fountain long dry, now it was little more than a wide place where paths converged. The trees had returned along with thick grasses in the open spaces and thicker brush in the shadows. It was still the center of the City, however, the place where news was shared, proclamations read, and advances celebrated. When Kendella's power plant had come online, the plaza erupted with parties for days.

Electricity had changed the City. Little by little, buildings new and old were configured to take advantage of it. Power snaked out to some buildings and even to a few clusters of homes the Loca had built. There weren't many machines that could use power, most having long been reduced to rust. Lightbulbs were almost impossible to come by, but the Loca were inventive and soon, bit by bit, cobbled parts reinvigorated The After.

After an hour's walk, the group stopped under towering trees beside the trail to eat and drink. Sunlight played on the grasses. Butterflies, or what looked like butterflies, flitted between the trees. Barth sat propped up beneath a large pine. He was fading and hadn't said a thing all morning.

"I don't think Barth will make it much further. We've got to let him rest," said Jen. "Frenz, Big Rod, you stay here with Barth. When he revives, get him back to that crater; we don't know what's in these woods, and you'll be safer there. Markus and I will head on into the City. We'll find food and water and be back by nightfall with help for Barth if we can find it. You good with that?" Jen asked, looking at Frenz and Big Rod. She had taken back the reins.

"Agreed," said Frenz. "Here, take one of the water bags; we can all use water. We'll take care of Barth."

"All right then. Markus, come with me." Jen stood, eyed the way forward, and stepped onto the path through the forest. "This way," she said. White butterflies followed.

17

Ruby heard someone talking. She stopped and stepped from the path into the shadows. What accent was this? They were not Loca, and it would not do to be found on the path unarmed if they were dangerous. Better to be safe and let them pass unseen.

"When I was here years ago, there were several who practiced the medical arts, healers like in the village. We need to find one for Barth," said one of them, a woman. "And food and water. We're almost out of both."

From the shadows, Ruby watched them pass. They were thin, filthy, not dressed for fighting, and looked like beggars. They were no threat. She stepped out onto the path behind them.

"I can help you," she said.

The voice behind them startled Markus and Jen, who spun to face it. The woman was tall, slender, the color of well-roasted coffee. Her face was decorated with scars. "You need help?" she said.

Jen looked the woman up and down. "Yes. We do. One of our group is injured. Do you know of a healer who can help him? Infection has set in and he's feverish."

Ruby stepped closer. Her shaved head glistened.

"I'm Ruby, and yes, we have a healer in the City. You're not from here, are you?"

Markus eyed her closely. He'd never seen anyone quite like this. Her blueberry-blue tunic was open to the waist, belted. "No," he said, "we're not. We were ambushed on the way here. Our friend was shot in the leg, and we're almost out of food and water." He hefted the almost-empty water bag. "This is Jen. I'm Markus."

Still wary, Ruby asked, "How many are you? Where's your injured friend?"

"There were six of us; now there're five. One was kidnapped by the man who shot Barth." This was indeed the most interesting woman Markus had ever seen. He stepped closer. "We're sure he brought her to the City, and we've got to find her, but first we need to see to Barth. He's with our friends who stayed to take care of him…back there." Markus pointed back up the trail.

"Oh," said Ruby. "I can take you to the healer. He'll be in his clinic. Name's Owen. It's this way."

Ruby immediately strode in front of Jen to

Markus's side. "Where are you from?" she asked. They started down the well-beaten path. Jen, amused, followed.

"We're from a village on the other side of the plain, Jen's Place. It's in a woodland. It's beautiful, and it's safe; the A-Eye have never attacked us. On the plain, they were everywhere. Do you have them here? We haven't seen any since we got here."

"No, they stay below the plateau and don't usually come to the City. When they do, though..." She stopped walking and faced Markus. Jen stopped as well.

"My father was killed by A-Eye when I was small. I was too young to remember, but they killed many of our people, my father included."

"I'm sorry," said Markus. "I never knew my parents or even what happened to them. Sophie, the girl who was kidnapped, and I moved around between families. We never had one of our own."

"Sophie? Is she your sister?"

"No, but sometimes it feels like it. We've been together since we were little. Now we work together. I'm worried about her." Markus glanced back at Jen, who stood listening, arms folded.

"She was kidnapped on your way here? Who took her?"

"A man named Luther. He's a liar and a thief. First, he stole our food and water, then ambushed us, shot Barth, and took Sophie. We're sure he's brought her here. He's looking for the same man we are, Albright."

Ruby brightened. "Albright! I know him! In fact, I worked for him. Well, I guess I still work for him. I'm just…on vacation." Ruby searched the ground, then looked up. "Actually, he fired me. Told me not to come back until I could…well, let's just say I'm on vacation…for a bit."

"You know Albright?" asked Jen, stepping up to join them. "Can you take us to him when we've seen to Barth?

"Sure, I can do that. He works in the Hilto. It's near the center of the City not too far from the clinic. He studies there, has his workshop. Lives there too."

Jen looked at Markus. *What luck!*

"Great! When we've seen to Barth and gotten food and water, we'd be most grateful if you could take us to him."

"Of course. Follow me."

Ruby led them into the City center, where stores were clustered along the path near the plaza. Some were in buildings with signs hung out front proclaiming their wares. Others were set up under awnings in front of buildings beyond repair. Loca milled about, shopping. Markus raised an eyebrow at Jen; he'd never seen such a place, colorful and busy. So different from the village.

Ruby took them to buy bread from a bakery and rabbit jerky and some fruit from a store that sold such.

"How can we repay you for these things?" asked Jen. "In our village, we barter for them. What do you do here?"

"Oh, we barter for them too, but sometimes we use these." Ruby reached into a pocket and held out small plastic beads, some red, some green. "I have enough from working with Albright. Don't worry about it. We'll stop for water after we find Owen. No need to lug a full water bag around until we return to your friends."

Soon enough, they found the healer's place. It was nestled just off the plaza in what was left of a building reinforced with stout lumber. Outside were benches for those waiting for attention. Inside were cots for the injured and two wooden tables for surgery. In a corner was a large cupboard stocked with vessels of liquid and powders, and from the ceiling hung bunches of dried herbs. In the center, bent over a man whose arm was gashed, was Owen, short, thick, and balding, a white, unruly fringe around his head. He was dressed in a gray tunic and leggings. A red sash was tied around his left arm, the sign of a healer.

"Owen?" said Ruby.

"Just a minute," he replied, not looking over his shoulder. "Let me finish here. Come back in a bit or wait here," he said, pointing to several chairs along a wall to the right.

"We'll be back," said Ruby, leading Markus and Jen outside. "I don't like the smell of that place—too much like death. Let's sit out here." She led them to what remained of the dry fountain in the center of the plaza. They sat on the low stone wall surrounding it.

"Ruby, how many people live in the City? How do you sustain yourselves? I didn't see any fields on our way here. Where do you get your food?" asked Jen.

"Our gardens are on the other side of the City, closer to water. We send some of it from the river into the fields. We even raise animals near there—rabbits, fowl, whatever we've been able to capture from the forest."

"And last night, before we camped, we saw what we thought was fire among the buildings. It was strange, blue, not red or yellow. What was that?"

Ruby sat erect, proud. "Those are lights, electric lights…powered by the power plant. My mother runs the plant. She learned how from books and brought the old power plant back to life. It's from The Before. It makes electricity."

Jen and Markus looked at each other, amazed. "What is it? What's electricity?" asked Jen.

"Electricity is like…invisible water that makes things go. Turbines make it from the river that flows through the dam on the south side of the City. We're still working on running it out into the City. There're not that many things that can use it, but it's a start. My mother is well known for making it work," said Ruby with pride.

Jen tried to imagine what the village would be like if it had electricity. She couldn't. "I'd love to meet your mother and see the power plant. Perhaps we can do that after our business here is done."

"Sure. How long do you think you'll be in the City?" Ruby said, stealing a glance at Markus.

"We'll need to get our strength back, and Barth will need time to heal. We have some business to take care of, then we'll go back to the village. My people need me," replied Jen. "It's a hard trip back."

"Yes, of course." Ruby looked toward the clinic. "Let's see if Owen's free." She jumped from her seat on the fountain's wall and brushed off her blue tunic. "And if he can see to your friend."

18

Luther flung the water bag at Sophie's feet. Still bound, she couldn't drink until he'd untied her hands. She drank once, then again. Water splashed on the plassik box at her feet.

"Thanks." *I hate to thank him for anything.*

"You're welcome. I'll get something to eat tomorrow. By the way, I'll be seeing Albright then. What do you think of that?" said Luther with a smug smile.

"It's no concern of mine," barked Sophie. "I don't care."

"You should care, Sophie. You may have a role in my 'negotiation' with Albright. I'm sure a pretty girl like you would interest him. In trade." He patted her on the head.

Sophie jerked away and rolled her eyes. *Is there no end to his filthy plans? Please gods, let me have his gun so I can end him!*

"Luther, what do you think you'll accomplish by finding Albright? This stupid idea of yours, that the A-Eye can return us to The Before…it makes no sense. That won't ever happen."

Luther beamed. "Oh, ye of little faith! The Prophet said it would be so, and it will be. The A-Eye caused all this, and they can repair it. I just have to convince them to do so." He took her hands and retied her at the wrists after she'd knotted the rope around one of them.

"You're delusional, Luther. And what does any of that have to do with this?" she asked, kicking the plassik box with her foot. "You don't know what's in here. Why would Albright care what it is?"

"We'll find out, won't we?" said Luther with a sneer.

"He was a strange one," said Kendella. "Said he and others had walked across the plain. Can you imagine? Most of his companions are dead. All he wanted was to have his water bag filled. And did I tell you he has only one hand?"

"Did he say why he was here?" asked Louis as he eyed the big gauges.

"Yeah, he wants to see Albright. I told him I'd take him to him. He should be back today sometime.

If you hear someone calling my name, it'll be him. In the meantime, help me with this, will you?"

Louis ambled over, holding a sizable wrench that he slid over a valve casing. Kendella grabbed the wheel, saying, "Okay, hold it," and twisted it hard to the left. "There. That ought to do it."

"I don't know. There was just something odd about the guy. Guess I'll find out more when he shows up today, if he does," she said.

Luther appeared in the late afternoon, calling Kendella's name through the open door to the power plant. Coming up from a lower floor, she found him waiting just outside the plant. He was alone.

"You didn't bring your companions?" asked Kendella, looking behind him.

"No, they're still too weak. *She's* too weak, I should say," said Luther. "After I get her something to eat and she's a little stronger, I'll bring her here. First, though, I'd like to see Albright."

"All right. I can take you now." *Interesting priority. Wonder why seeing Albright is more important than helping his "companion."*

Owen welcomed Ruby and the visitors and, hearing of Barth's plight, agreed to go with them back to the outskirts of the City. "Just let me get my things," he said. He packed a kit, and they set off past the dry fountain, stopping once at a water shop to fill the bag.

"How long have you been a healer, Owen?" asked Jen as they walked through the City.

"I was born into it. My father and his father were both healers, and theirs before them back to before The After. It's all I've ever known."

"Thank you for agreeing to come with us to see Barth. His wound was clean; the buddet passed through his leg and hit no bone, but the wound's become infected. He's feverish and weaker by the day," said Jen.

She led them back to the crater on the edge of the City where Frenz, Big Rod, and Barth were waiting. Frenz and Big Rod had brought Barth to the bottom, where he was stretched out, head on a near-empty water bag. The rag wrapped around his wound was dark with crusted blood. He was sweating.

Owen cleaned Barth's wound, wrapped it, gave Barth a liquid to drink, and handed a small, black-stoppered jug to Jen. "This will bring his fever down. Give him a drink four times a day. As soon as he is able, bring him to the clinic where he can rest and heal."

Barth's eyes were red and his complexion pale. His long beard was matted and tangled. "Thank you," was all he could say.

"How can we repay you?" said Jen.

"We'll figure that out when he's in the clinic.

There are always things that need to be done there. I'll give it some thought."

"Perhaps I should stay here to lead you back to the clinic when he's able to travel," said Ruby, eyeing Markus. "Then I can take you to Albright's. It's not far from there."

"If you wish," said Jen. "You'll be sleeping rough, though."

"It won't be the first time! I brought my own food and have extra water. Shouldn't be a burden."

"All right then," said Jen. "Stay." She turned and said, "Owen, thank you. We should see you in a few days."

Owen said his goodbyes and left. Jen hovered around Barth while Markus and Ruby moved up to the top of the crater. Frenz and Big Rod put together a fire.

"Is that the sign of your tribe?" Ruby pointed to the scab on Markus's ankle. They sat cross-legged on the ground, facing each other. Darkness was not far off.

"What? No. I cut myself in the foothills on the way here. What do you mean, 'tribe'?"

"Here, we identify ourselves and the tribe we belong to by these." She touched the keloid swirls on her cheeks. "It says who you are, who you run with, your friends. Or at least to the Loca that are young. The older ones, our parents and grandparents…" She rolled her eyes. "…think they're terrible. We see them as beautiful decorations that signify we belong to a group, our tribe."

Markus looked again at Ruby's face. *The pattern is beautiful*, he thought, *but not something I'd ever want to do. She's such a...strange woman. Pretty, but strange.*

"My mother and Doritz, my grandmother, especially, think I've ruined my looks and my future. They're so...controlling. I hate it here!" she fumed.

They sat on the edge of the crater. Below them, Jen, Barth, Frenz, and Big Rod huddled around the fire. It had gotten chilly in the early evening.

"Do you ever feel that way, Markus, like your life wasn't your own, that everything you did had to be what someone else wanted you to do?"

"I guess I've never thought about it. My life in the village is pretty...I don't know, simple. Sophie and I scavenge the pits that aren't too far away and use the things we find to barter for what we need. Nobody tells us what to do. We've been on our own for a long time."

"I envy you," said Ruby. She had inched closer to Markus, to sit by his side. Heat radiated from her body, and Markus couldn't help but glance beneath the tunic that hung open to her waist.

"You and Sophie. You said you'd been raised together and now work together." Ruby looked at Markus, her dark eyes shining. "Is there more to it than that? Are you...a couple?"

Markus blanched at the question. This was the

heart of the matter for him. Were they a couple? What did he want them to be? He was slow to answer.

"We've been together since we were children, grew up together. I never thought of her as anything more than a sister. Now...I don't know what I think."

Ruby took Markus's hand. He turned to look at her—really look at her.

A-EYE

19

Two days after Owen had given him the first dose, Barth felt better. In fact, despite Jen's admonishment, he sat up and began looking for his crossbow and hide armor. "I'm ready," he said.

Jen pushed him back down on his sleeping pallet. "No, you're not, Barth. You've been shot. You've had a fever and been delirious. The medicine the healer gave you is working, but you're not well enough to walk into the City. Let's give it another day, okay? You need it."

Barth nodded and lay back down after Jen gave him another swallow of the healer's medicine. He'd slept straight through the past two days. And he had dreamed. The dreams were different from his visions; they were lucid, rapid, and confusing. He could only recall bits of them, which made interpreting them in the light of day almost impossible. This he did remember, however: blue fire.

To the rest of the group, Jen said, "We've got enough food and water for another day or two here, then we'll go into the City. Barth's better, but he still needs to get his strength back. Ruby, can you stay another day before guiding us back to Owen's?"

"Sure. I'm here for whatever you ask of me."

"When we get into the City, we'll take Barth to the healer's and then go to Albright's?" Frenz asked.

"Yes, Ruby can take us to him," said Jen. "I imagine Luther has already seen Albright unless Sophie slowed him down. Regardless, Albright can help us. I'm sure he will." *Albright. It's been so many years. I don't know what he'll think when we meet. He'll remember me, I'm sure, but will he remember the cold goodbye? Will he be ashamed, sad, that nothing more happened between us? I have no idea what to expect, of him, of me. No idea.*

Markus and Ruby walked into the surrounding brush looking for berries. It was that time of year when the punkinberries ripened. The foothills had given way to more vegetation and a few small trees. In the scrub, the bright orange berries were easy to spot. Markus brought a bag they'd take back to the rest of the group when full. The day was mild, but a change in the light hinted at the coming fall.

"Markus, when we go back into the City, would it

be okay if I stayed with you—your group? I'd like to help however I can, help you find Luther...and Sophie."

"Sure. Jen will make that call, though. She's our leader. Something's been on her mind; the closer we've gotten to the City, the more preoccupied she's become. I know she's been worried about Barth, but it's something else too. Whoa! Look at that! Loaded with berries."

Ruby held the bag open while Markus rummaged in the bush to pick the fat berries. He threw one into his mouth. "Wow! These are so good! I've never had one before; they don't grow around the village. Guess it's the wrong climate or something." In no time, the bag was full of orange delights.

"So, you'll talk to Jen and make sure it's all right?" Ruby asked. "When we get back, you can meet my mom, K. She's something! She and Louis run the hydroelectric plant that generates power. It's from The Before. She found it and got it going again. If she wasn't such a pain, I'd be proud of her. Well, I *am* proud of her, but she's so exasperating. I'm grown, but she treats me like a kid. And Doritz is even worse. I can't wait to get out of here."

"Really? You'd leave the City? And go where? What would you do?"

"I don't know for sure. I only know I want to find someplace new, be someone new. You know?" Ruby scuffed the earth with her shoe and looked up at Markus.

He ran his fingers through his hair. "I guess. I can't imagine ever leaving the village, the people…but I can't imagine scavenging for the rest of my life either. Frenz and Big Rod—scrambling forever for their next find—that's not how I want to end up."

He popped a punkinberry into his mouth. "Scavenging's not hard work. Dirty, yeah, but not that hard. It's just so unpredictable." He faced Ruby. "Others in the village my age, though, they make things, grow things. They *do* things. I don't have those skills. I'd be starting over to find…whatever it is. Scavenging's all I've ever done, and it's what's kept us going."

Us.

Markus lowered the bag. "That's the other thing: Sophie. I can't imagine leaving her by herself." They were both silent for a moment.

"It won't be easy, leaving the City, Ruby. Crossing the plain was rough, and it's dangerous. You'd have to do that to get anywhere new, wouldn't you?"

"Yeah, I'd need someone to come with me," said Ruby as she looked at Markus. He was busy eating punkinberries.

Sophie was thirsty and hungry. Again, Luther had been gone for hours. The water bag lay beside her but did her no good; she was tightly bound. *He's up to some-thing. He got this water from somewhere, which means he found someone in the City to help him, maybe take him to Albright. Is he serious about offering me up for what he wants? Would Albright take a deal like that? Is he that kind of man?*

She rubbed her itching nose with her shoulder. *Don't know, but I know that it'll be up to me to get out of this mess. My friends are who-knows-where and have other things on their plate…like helping Barth. If I'm going to get free, it's up to me.* She smiled at the rhyme, pondering. *Or I can make him think I'm more trouble than I'm worth, and he'll let me go. How big of a bitch can I be?* She smiled. *A real bitch!*

Luther trailed Kendella through the City. It was nothing like he'd expected. The ones he'd visited with the Prophet had been in much worse shape. Of course, they were up north where the wind and weather kept the ground hard and dry when it wasn't covered with snow. Here it was completely different, pleasant almost. The tall trees that had matured through the years brought shade and wildlife like he'd never seen. Birds! Many of the buildings had been partially reconstructed, although most were at ground level; only a few taller ones remained. The Loca had built houses of varying styles throughout the City, some just elaborate lean-tos, some built of stone from the old buildings. Children ran through the trees and along the paths, laughing. Luther wondered what it had been like in The Before.

"K, how long have you known Albright?" Luther asked.

"For years. I was in my teens when he came here. He was gorgeous, mysterious, and seemed disconnected from the day-to-day world. After a while, he took over the Hilto building. It was one of the few buildings with two stories; still is. At first, he spent his time interviewing Loca, finding out where information was kept, such as it was. That was what he was interested in, Hisry. He wanted to know everything about The Before. After I discovered the Library, he spent months down there. Once I had the power plant running, he ran power to the Hilto so he could continue his work more easily. Then he found something called 'microfilm' and a machine that read it. He became very excited about that. Said it opened a lot of doors for him.

"Don't see too much of him now. He mostly stays in the Hilto—he lives there on the second floor. Has what he calls his lab on the first floor."

"Ummm." Luther was only mildly interested in all this. What was more important was what Albright could tell him and where to find A-Eye. That was what mattered.

He still had to figure out what part Sophie would play in getting Albright to give him what he wanted. How he could use her to bargain was yet to be determined. Having her in his pocket was enough right now. It didn't look like his dream of a glorious life together would happen, but he'd get what he wanted out of her, one way or another.

"We're here," said Kendella, pointing at a two-story building. Over the entrance, the letters hammered into stone spelled out H-I-L-T-O.

20

Albright sat at a wooden table in the rear of his lab. A single electric light burned beside him, casting one side in shadow. Gray dreadlocks hung down his back, parting when he turned at the sound of visitors.

"Albright, there's someone to see you," said Kendella.

The room was spacious and filled to the brim with cabinets, tables, boxes, and, up against another wall, a microfilm reader. Cables drooped from the ceiling, bringing power.

"Oh?" said Albright, turning in his chair. A tall, very dark-skinned man, he wore a long brown kaftan and sandals. A small, flat, silver moon hung from his neck on a thin chain. "And you are?" he asked, rising. He stepped toward Luther, towering over him, and smiled, teeth blazingly white, eyes as black as a snake's.

"Uh, I'm Luther. Come from across the plain to see you. Have some things you may be interested in. And I believe you have information I need."

Albright took in the visitor: gaunt, shoeless, dirty. Yes, a traveler. One sleeve hung empty. "Well then, have a seat. Thank you, K." Albright pointed Luther to a chair and, with a twitch of his wrist, dismissed Kendella.

"Always happy to see a new face here. You say you crossed the plain? Hard business, that."

Luther nodded.

"What can I do for you?" asked Albright, still standing.

"I have a box, a large plassik box from a pit on the other side of the plain. Inside is something that could be of great value, but the box is impossible to open. If you can do that, you can have what's inside. In exchange, I'd like some information."

"What sort of information?"

"Oh, we'll get to that after you tell me if you can open the box. Fair enough?"

Albright nodded. "Why do you think I'd be interested in what's inside this box?" he asked, still standing.

"Because it came from the pits near the NORAD installations. This is what I was told."

"NORAD. The defense organization. And who told you this? For that matter, how did you get the box?"

"I'm a trader by profession," Luther lied. "I come across interesting things, and when I do, I dig to find out more about them—their 'provenance,' I believe it's called. In this case, the person who found it told me the box was the original property of the NORAD Command. Because it's been impossible to open, that lends authority to the NORAD connection. They would have that kind of protective technology, wouldn't they?"

"And how did you get the box? Did you buy it?"

"I bartered for it, as is my custom, just as I wish to barter with you for the information I need."

"I see," said Albright, looking at Luther's empty sleeve. "And how did you come to lose your hand?"

"Sometimes, in my line of work, things don't go as planned. This was the outcome of a barter gone awry. Thugs robbed me, took what they wanted, but left me this." He pulled back his sleeve.

"And where is this box? May I see it?"

"It's with a companion. This is my first time in the City and not knowing what I'd find here, or if I'd even find you, I thought it best to leave it in a safe place."

"And how did you come to find me? Why do you think I can help you open the box, or that I'd be interested in what's inside?"

"Your reputation precedes you."

Albright eyed his guest, wary of flattery. "Tell me a bit about yourself, Luther. What's your background?

Where are you from? How did you get into the bartering trade?"

At this, Luther began spewing out one lie after another. He was raised on the West Coast and had traveled all over what had once been Canada and most of what had been the United States. Along the way, he began acquiring things for barter, and that brought him to today's business.

"I was also a religious devotee for a while and traveled much in the northern areas. Are you familiar with the Prophet?"

"No, can't say I am."

"Brilliant man, brilliant. Foresaw so many things, including a return to The Before."

Albright had taken a seat during Luther's ramblings and now sat up straighter. "Umm. I'm surprised I haven't heard of him as that's also an interest of mine, the exchange between The Before and The After. How is it that this Prophet believed we could return to The Before?"

"That matter involves the information I believe you can provide me. We can discuss that further after you confirm you can open the box. Agreed?"

Albright nodded, and after more pleasantries he showed his guest to the door. *Strange. How many people know about NORAD—what it was—and how many of those might know about its possible connection to the end of The Before? Strange.*

The trees along the path were thick in this part of the City. The further from the central plaza, the denser they got. *Wonder if this is like the village Jen and Sophie described?* thought Luther. He knew his way back to where he'd left Sophie, or thought he did. That's the problem with forests: when you're in them you can't see anything but the trees in front of you. One thing he hadn't seen was much wildlife aside from the birds. Kendella had talked a little about animals on the way to Albright's, but he hadn't been listening. Instead, he was thinking about how he would make his pitch to Albright. Had she said there were predators?

Albright: he's an odd one. Those questions… I think he bought my story. He certainly perked up when I mentioned NORAD. That was a stroke of genius, if I do say so. He doesn't seem like the type that would be interested in Sophie, though. What can I do with her? She's a weight and a liability. But oh, so lovely…

By the time Luther got back to where he'd left Sophie, it was nearly dark. He'd stopped at a bakery and stole small loaves while the shopkeeper was engaged with another customer. Untying her hands, he gave one to Sophie. Her legs remained hobbled, and she could have untied the rope given enough time, but not with Luther around. The gun was tucked into his belt.

"What did you do in the City?" she asked. "Find Albright?" She gnawed on the loaf.

Luther chewed his dinner; finally, "Yes."

"And did he agree to open the box?"

"Not yet, but he will." Luther turned to face her. "He'll see what I have and be hungry to get to what's inside. I'm sure of it." He paused and looked her in the eye. "I also don't think he'd be interested in you, you know, for any reason. Pity."

"So, there's no part for me in your stupid plan? Then how about letting me go, Luther?" Even as she said it, she knew that wasn't possible. He knew she'd expose him for the thief and liar he was. Her face darkened as she realized there could be only one outcome: He would never let her go, and would have the A-Eye kill her when he found them.

21

Barth stepped deliberately along the beaten path. He was much improved, but his leg couldn't bear all his considerable weight. Frenz had removed most of his hardened hide armor to lighten his load, but he still struggled and his tunic was damp with sweat.

"Barth, take your time. We're in no hurry," said Jen. Barth nodded, wincing with each step. He, Frenz, and Jen followed Markus and Ruby. She knew the way, and together they walked ahead.

"Markus, have you talked to Jen about my joining your group? I can be more than a guide through the City. I've worked with...well, *for*...Albright and can help with him. He can be stubborn...when he's not acting like he doesn't care. He's a hard one to figure out, and I've known him since I was little."

"No, I haven't had a chance to talk to Jen, but I can't imagine why she wouldn't take you up on your offer to help. None of us know the City like you do, and we can use all the help we can get."

"Good." Ruby took Markus's hand. He didn't resist.

Jen stepped beside Frenz and walked beside him. They dropped back from the others. "Frenz, when we find Luther, capturing him may not be easy, especially since he's armed. Barth's not at full strength, and none of the rest of us are really fighters. We can help, but we need someone to lead us, somebody experienced, someone a little more…physical. I know this isn't why you've come to the City, but will you help us when the time comes, you and Big Rod?"

"Yeah," said Frenz, nodding. "What's your plan? Do you have one?" *Again, I'm responsible for someone…but I can't not help them. They've got no chance by themselves against Luther, much less the A-Eye.*

"You know what they say, 'make plans and the gods laugh.' Beyond finding Luther and Sophie and hoping he has the box with him, we'll need to improvise. He'll have his firearm—I don't know with how many buddets—and that's the biggest problem. Without that, he'd be easy to overcome, but his gun raises the stakes."

"Big Rod and I have experience with armed men. We can take him. Just need to find him."

"Ruby will take us to Albright's after we get Barth to the clinic. We'll find out what he knows about

Luther, if he's been there. Albright's either going to help Luther locate the A-eye or not. Frankly, I can't imagine he'd want to help him, but what's in the plassik box could be an enticement. We'll know soon enough."

Owen had finished setting the lad's broken arm when the visitor rushed into the clinic. He didn't introduce himself, but to Owen, he needed no introduction. It was Luther, the creep Jen and the other newcomers had talked about, the man who'd shot Barth, stolen the plassik box, and kidnapped Sophie. Of this, Owen was certain.

Tugging on Owen's arm, Luther insisted he leave the clinic to see to a companion—a woman, he said, in distress. Owen got his kit together and followed Luther to a path leading to the edge of town. *If only there was a way to get word to Jen and her group. If there's not, then it will be up to me to free Sophie.*

"What's wrong with her?" asked Owen as they hurried along, trees bending over the well-worn trail.

"I don't know. At daybreak she began moaning, and her breathing was odd. She didn't respond to anything I did," said Luther. "I couldn't get her to open her eyes."

"Well, we'll see to her soon enough. Not to worry."

"She's here," said Luther, pointing to a small clearing not far off the path. Sophie was lying on her side, legs bound at the ankles, her hands tied in front of her. Her shift was filthy, her eyes were closed, and her breathing was labored.

"Has she eaten, had something to drink?" asked Owen as he bent over to examine Sophie. He spread one eye with his fingers and jerked when Sophie turned her blue eye toward him. Owen had his back to Luther, who wouldn't have seen that she was awake.

"When did she take ill?" asked Owen.

"This morning, right after she had some bread and water. She started moaning and twitching and fell over. I haven't been able to wake her."

"You had her bound like this?" Owen tugged at the ropes around her hands and ankles.

"Uh, yes. She…sleepwalks, walks in her sleep. I hobble her so she doesn't wander away. I don't know this area, and she'd be hard to find."

"I see," said Owen. "And is she a relative, a daughter?"

At this, Luther bristled. "Uh no, she's my…wife."

Owen was enjoying Luther's discomfort. "I need more water for her. Do you have a full water bag?"

Luther shook his head. "No, only what's in here."

Owen hefted the bag. "It won't be enough. Will you find more? I need to keep her cool. If her fever worsens, it could be fatal. I'm afraid she's ingested something poisonous. I need her to throw up whatever it is she ate." He handed Luther the water bag.

Luther took the water bag and looked at her again. "Okay. I'll be back as soon as I can. You're sure she can't go anywhere?"

"Oh, no, you can see she's terribly weak. She won't be moving from this spot."

Luther hurried off down the path, turning once to confirm Sophie's infirmity.

Owen leisurely inventoried the contents of his kit, glancing now and then at the path Luther took. *That should do it. He's gone.*

Bending over her, he said, "Sophie. You're Sophie, yes?"

She opened both eyes and turned her head to face him. "Yes. How do you know my name?"

"I've spent some time with Jen and her group. They spoke of you…and Luther. I recognized him when he came to my clinic. I'm Owen. The healer. Can you sit up?"

"Yes." Sophie rolled to her back and struggled to her elbows. "How did you know I wasn't ill?"

"Jen and Markus said you were clever. I figured you'd fooled Luther into thinking you were sick, hoping he'd go for help. Well, he did, and here I am."

Sophie sat up and began untying her ankles. "I gambled he still thinks there's a chance I'll change my mind about him, so he'd want to keep me alive…for now." She laughed. "The idiot."

She turned to him then. "How are my friends, Jen, Barth? How's Barth? Is he why you met them, to tend to him? And Markus? How's Markus?"

"Barth should be well on his way to recovering by now. I saw him three days ago. Jen said when he was well enough, they'd come to my clinic in the City. Can you walk, or were you ever at all ill?"

"I'm weak—haven't had much to eat—but aside from that, I'm fine. If you think they're in the City, then let's go there," she said, rising. "We should stay off the path in case Luther comes back."

Owen bent to untie the rope around Sophie's ankles when Luther's revolver came down on the back of his head. Hard.

22

Hearing the bells, Ruby turned and waved for her cohorts to move to the side of the path. "Let the cart pass," she said.

From behind them, a cart drew near, pulled by a small man and a stout woman; its thin wooden wheels squeaked loudly. "Morning," said the woman as she drew the cart to a stop. "Going into the City? That big fellow need a lift?" she said, eyeing Barth. "We've got room, and he shouldn't be much of a problem."

"Yes, and yes," said Jen. "Barth is recovering from…an injury. We're taking him to the healer's clinic. Would be much obliged if he could make the rest of the way in your cart."

"Come on then. Pierce, help that fellow in and show him where to sit, so we stay balanced."

Big Rod and the man helped Barth climb into the cart, where he sat in the center. Frenz laid his armor hides and crossbow beside him. Barth nodded, and the cart began to roll, the man and woman straining against their yokes.

"Whoa, he's a load," the woman said, holding out the cart harness to Frenz. "Think you could help us out here?"

"Happy to," said Frenz. "Ruby, can you help?" She nodded and stepped into the harness beside him.

"Glad you came along," said Big Rod to the woman who now walked beside him. "Barth's tough, but he's been through it. No reason to push it."

"After we get Barth to the clinic, we'll find Albright?" Frenz asked Jen as he strained against the yoke. She walked alongside the cart. "Then what?"

Jen rubbed her chin. "Depends on what we find at Albright's, whether Luther has been there yet, which I suspect he has. We'll just have to see."

Luther finished tying up Owen and looked at Sophie. "I'll be back for you once I've met with Albright. Then we'll be off to find the A-Eye." With difficulty, he picked up the plassik box. "And you, Owen. Not to worry. Someone will probably find you after we've gone. You won't die here. Or maybe you will!" he said with a grin. Then he set off for Albright's.

Though it was always difficult to see deep in the forest, gray clouds now obscured what little sky remained. It smelled like it might rain. Sophie watched Luther disappear down the path. *Gods, I hate him.* The forest closed around them.

"Owen, are you married? Do you have a family?" They were both bound, tied to either side of a tall pine. Luther had left the open water bag between them from which, with effort, they could take sips.

"I was, and I did."

"What happened?"

"A-Eye. Just when we felt safe…we weren't."

"How long ago did you…lose them?"

"Twelve years ago. I needed to go to one of the villages north on the plateau. It was a beautiful day, and I took my wife and children. We'd be gone and back before dark. I suppose it was a family outing; I'm tied to the clinic for so much of the time. On the way home—I'd gotten herbs and other things for the clinic —we stopped to rest and give the children a chance to run about. Never gave a thought to the A-Eye; they stay below the foothills. We were totally unprepared.

"You know A-Eye have a distinctive sound when they travel, yes?" Sophie nodded, although Owen couldn't see her. "I heard it, that clanking noise, and knew what it was."

Owen stopped; words clogged his throat. He saw his wife, his children, roasted in the blue fire from the A-Eye.

Both were silent for a while, then Sophie said, "I'm so sorry you got dragged into this. Luther is…

he's the worst human being I've ever come across. And to top it off, he's suicidal. He thinks he can meet the A-Eye and convince them to restore The Before. I mean, how does that work? He's stupid...and crazy."

Owen nodded. "None of this is your fault, Sophie. I don't know what else I, or you, could have done. He fooled me when he left. I thought we were in the clear." He paused, thinking. Wanting to change the subject, he said, "The group you're traveling with, the villagers, who's the young man you asked about? Jen said you'd grown up together. What's he like?"

"His name is Markus, and yes, we grew up together. We work together. He's always felt like a brother to me —but the way I feel about him now is different."

"Different how?" Owen turned to face her as best he could.

"I've always liked him, always liked being with him. He's funny, brave, and caring in a way a lot of men aren't. I guess that's it: He's a man now, not the boy I've known all my life. Now it's...different; I miss him. I want to be with him."

"The way you feel about him has changed?"

"Yeah. He's all I've thought about during this... whatever this is with Luther." Sophie strained against the ropes and glanced up at the darkening sky. "I don't know when—or if—I'll ever see him again."

"Sounds like you're falling in love, Sophie. To feel that way about someone who's first been a dear friend is rare…and lucky. My wife and I were like that. We'd been friends our whole lives, had grown up together, but then I fell in love with her and wanted more. Is that what you feel?"

"I guess so. Yes. And it scares me. I've never felt like this about anyone. What if he doesn't feel the same way, still thinks of me as a sister? I don't know if I could stand that."

Owen turned as far as he could toward her, stretching against the ropes. "Sophie, love takes courage. Always. It means opening your heart, knowing you could get hurt, but being willing to take that risk. Are you willing to do that?"

Sophie was quiet for a moment. "Yes."

Barth sat on a bench by the front door of the clinic, his injured leg stretched before him. Frenz, Ruby, Barth, and the cart had gotten to the clinic before Jen and Big Rod. After goodbyes, the cart continued on its way.

"He's not here," said Barth as Jen walked to him. "They say he hurried off somewhere and hasn't been seen since."

"He'll be back," said Jen. "Best you find a spot inside and get some rest. That leg won't mend without it," she said, pointing at the seeping bandage. "Ruby will take us to Albright's, and we'll find out what's what and decide what to do next."

Barth started to object but saw it would be of no use. His leg *was* better, but... Big Rod and Ruby helped him into the clinic, where he found a cot.

"Ruby, once we get to Albright's, will you go in and see if Luther's there or has been?" asked Jen. "If he is there, he won't know you and won't be suspicious. We'll find someplace nearby and wait for you. Depending on what you find, we'll figure out what to do next. Okay?"

They walked through the City until Ruby stopped them. She pointed: "That's the Hilto, Albright's place. Stay here. I'll check on Luther." She set off and disappeared into its gaping entrance, but not before smiling at Markus. The others stepped into an alley facing the Hilto and stood behind thick shrubs at its entrance.

"If he's there, what's the plan?" Markus asked.

"Frenz, you're in the lead here. What do we do?" asked Jen.

"If Ruby tells us he's inside, we'll spread out to cover the front door and wait until he comes out; then we'll take him." He and Big Rod cocked their crossbows.

Presently, Ruby appeared and walked to them. "He's not there, but Albright said he's coming back. And soon."

23

Frenz's trap was simple enough. From the alley they could see the Hilto's doorway. When Luther came out and was clear of the entrance, Frenz and Big Rod would take him by surprise. If they acted quickly enough, caught between both of them, Luther wouldn't have a chance to wield his firearm. If he somehow escaped, they'd deal with that then.

"He's got his firearm and a few buddets. Frenz, your and Big Rod's crossbows, can they bring him down before he can shoot?" asked Jen.

Frenz nodded. "If we're lucky, but we don't want to kill him. He's the only one who knows where Sophie is."

Markus winced at the thought.

"Ruby, will you ask Albright to come here?" asked Jen. "It's his place, and he should know what we're doing and why. Don't want anyone in there—or him —to get hurt."

"Yes. Now?"

Jen nodded, and Ruby headed back to the Hilto.

Jen was as nervous as she'd ever been. Albright. How many years had it been since she'd seen him? Would he remember her the way she remembered him? *If we make it through this, I've got to talk to him... about us.*

Albright emerged from the Hilto first, followed by Ruby. He was thinner and grayer than Jen had last seen him but was still...magnificent. He strode to the group and immediately addressed Frenz, paying no attention to the others.

"Ruby said you wanted to see me, and that you're here for Luther. Why?" he asked.

Frenz glanced in Jen's direction and said, "My friends have come across the plain to see you. Luther ambushed them in the foothills and stole that box, shot one of their men, and kidnapped one of their women. I'm Frenz, and I'm helping them. Luther has a gun, so getting the girl and the box will be tricky. I believe you know Jen?"

Albright turned and, for the first time, saw her. Jen stepped forward; she nodded, her body stiffening.

"Albright," was all she could say.

He stared. A small smile played on his lips. "Jen. It's good to see you. It's been a long time, and you've come far. How can I help?"

"Luther is coming to you with the plassik box, yes? He'll ask you where the A-Eye are so he can parlay with them. Crazy, I know, but play along with it. Tell him where he can find them, but keep the box under some pretense and let him leave. When he does, we'll take him. He has a gun, but we have these," she said, pointing at Frenz's crossbow. "That's all we ask."

"That I can do."

"Thank you. We hope that after we catch him, he'll tell us where the girl is. If he doesn't, we could use your help in finding her. You know the City; we don't."

"One thing at a time, Jen. Let's see how your plan plays out. After, we'll talk more. If I can help then, I will." His smile broadened a bit. "It's good to see you. You look well." His eyes lingered on her, then he turned and walked back into the Hilto.

Frenz's plan should have worked, could have worked, didn't work. At dusk, Luther came to the Hilto with the box under his good arm and showed it to Albright. While they talked, he shook what was inside like a piece of cheese in a trap, again mentioning the supposed connection to **NORAD**. Albright held it to the light on his desk to make out the blue or green thing inside. Luther went on and on about meeting with the A-Eye and what he intended to do. He only needed to know exactly where they were and now many; that's what he wanted. If Albright could open it, he could have what was in the box. Albright said he could, but it would take some time. Would Luther leave it with him?

With that agreed to, Albright drew a detailed map to the A-Eye nest, and Luther left the Hilto, heading toward the plaza. Just outside the door was where the plan fell apart.

Luther had taken a dozen steps when Frenz stepped out from an alley and shouted, "Luther. Stop right there!" Big Rod moved behind him from out of the shadows, standing some meters away, crossbow in hand. Luther turned to face one, then the other, and his eyes went wide when Jen joined Big Rod.

"Well now! Who's this?" he said, glancing at Jen. "Friends of the heathens? And they made it to the City? Amazing! Did the brute not make it? So sorry!" He looked from Frenz to Big Rod, smiling, and pulled the revolver from under his belt. "Crossbows. How brave!"

He aimed at Big Rod but then swung to Frenz, the bigger target, and fired. The buddet slammed into the building behind Frenz as he ducked for cover. Big Rod raised his crossbow and let loose a bolt. It went wide. Frenz pulled his crossbow up, but before he could fire, Luther turned and ran, dodging and running low to the ground. Markus came running from behind the Hilto when he heard the commotion and could only watch as Luther sprinted away toward the forest. Before he disappeared, he slowed once and yelled back, "If you follow me, you'll never see Sophie again." No one followed him.

Standing outside the Hilto, Jen asked, "Ruby, where is he going? Where are the A-Eye?" She was frustrated but not surprised by Luther's escape, given that he had the gun.

"The A-Eye have a place…we call it their 'nest.' We don't know what they do there, but we think they repair themselves and make more A-Eye. It's below the foothills on the edge of the plain in a place scooped out of the side of a hill. That's where they are."

"We need more help to find him and take him when we do," said Frenz. "Though he'll want to, Barth shouldn't come with us. He's still too weak. Ruby, you mentioned your mother. Would she help us? Are there others who could?"

"I'm sure she'll help. She's smart and knows the A-Eye. As for others, I don't know. Do we have enough time to gather an army? That's what we'd need against the A-Eye."

"No, Luther already has a head start on us. Besides, we're not going there to fight the A-Eye, but to get Sophie back. If we're lucky, we won't engage with the A-Eye. How long will it take us to get there, Ruby?"

"It's a two-day journey; we'll need supplies, water, food." She ticked those off on her fingers.

"Okay. Big Rod and Markus, come with me," said Jen. "We'll get what we need. Frenz, go with Ruby and see if her mother will come with us. We'll meet to leave from the clinic at daybreak."

Jen, Markus, and Big Rod reclaimed their water bags. They stopped at the clinic to tell Barth the plan, and that he wasn't coming with them. As expected, he protested. Frenz gave Jen the green and red beads he'd taken off Clapper, so they had what was used for money. They went to buy bread, rabbit jerky, fruit, and whatever else they could find.

Ruby led Frenz past the plaza to the power plant. She leaned into the open door and called for her mother. Kendella called back, "Coming."

She walked up the stairs to the door, wiping her hands on a rag. Even glistening with sweat and her hair stuck to her wet forehead, she was an attractive woman. Frenz could only stare.

"Mom, this is Frenz."

Frenz stuck out his hand but withdrew it, seeing Kendella's greasy hand.

"Yeah, sorry," she said. "I'm Kendella. Friends call me K. Nice to meet you."

"Mom, this isn't a social call. We need your help. A whacko kidnapped one of Frenz's friends and is taking her to the A-Eye camp. We've got to get her back before they get there. Like, right now. Can you help us—me and the others?"

"What? When? You mean *now* now? How many are you? And how do you know these people?"

"I met them on their way into the City. They're from a village on the other side of the plain. Long story. They came to see Albright. I'm leading them to the A-Eye, and we can use your help."

"Why is the friend being taken to the A-Eye?"

"Like I said, long story. Will you come? We're leaving from the plaza at first light."

"Ruby, I've got responsibilities here. This place doesn't run itself," said Kendella, looking back over her shoulder.

"Mom. They need your help. *I* need your help! Please."

"You mentioned Albright. What's he got to do with this?"

"Mom, we don't have time to go into all that. Just say you'll help us!"

"Won't we need supplies, food, water?"

"That's being taken care of. Mom, please! I don't ask you for much."

Kendella hadn't taken her eyes off Frenz, who hadn't taken his off her. "Okay," she said and yelled for Louis.

24

The sky had lowered, and the clouds darkened. A light mist fell. Sophie and Owen had drifted off to sleep, each hugging themselves into a ball, trying to stay warm.

"Move it!" Luther nudged Sophie in the thigh. "We need to get going." He poked her again.

"Hey," yelled Sophie. "I heard you the first time!"

"Get to it then. We've got a good way to go to reach the A-Eye."

"What? You really are going to the A-Eye? That's madness! Are you crazy?" asked Owen as he unwound.

"Absolutely, we're going. This will be the beginning of the end of The After. I've got a map, and we have supplies. Up," he said, pointing at Sophie.

"In the dark? In this weather? You *are* crazy," mumbled Sophie. She stood, stretched as much as she could with bound hands, and, glancing at Owen, said, "You'll be okay here, Owen?"

"He'll be fine," inserted Luther. "Don't worry about him. Someone will find him soon enough. Now get going. Take these." He handed Sophie a full water bag and another bag of bread and rabbit jerky that he'd stolen. Gun in hand, he marched her back onto the path. They headed for the foothills as darkness fell.

Owen watched, slowly shaking his head. *This won't end well.*

Following the trail through the foothills took time. Luther referred constantly to the map he'd gotten from Albright. In the soft moonlight, it was not impossible to read. The spot where the A-Eye congregated had a name, but Luther couldn't read Albright's handwriting.

Sophie's bitching was relentless. "Luther, how can you believe the A-Eye won't just burn us? They don't know you, don't know what you want. You won't be able to open your mouth before you get roasted."

Luther was so tired of it. "I've told you, the Prophet established a rapport with them. They're all connected somehow, like ants. They'll recognize me." He rubbed his stubbed arm against his chest. What he didn't say was how his last encounter with them had ended.

"I'm sure they'll sense what it is I want. They have the power to return us to The Before. I'm sure of it."

Sophie rolled her eyes. "You're delusional. And why am I here? What good can I do? Don't you think it would be easier if you let me go? I'll only be in the way. If, as you say, the A-Eye will know your intentions, great, but they don't know me, don't know mine. I could get us killed and not even know it."

"Just shut up, Sophie. Shut up."

They'd left the plateau and had started on a modest decline. The sky was beginning to lighten. They'd walked all night; it was not easy to do in the semi-dark.

"We're stopping here," said Luther, throwing down his bags against a boulder. "Find my firestarter, gather up whatever will burn from around here, and get a fire going. When you're done with the fire, tie your legs at the ankles, tight."

Sophie did as he commanded, hard as it was with her wrists bound. After she'd started the fire, she knotted her ankles. Luther rolled her over and kneeled on her shoulders while he retied her hands behind her. Not easy to do with one hand. He pulled up her legs and looped the rope from them to her hands, pulling it tighter when she protested. There wasn't much she could move.

"I'd say we're halfway there. We'll rest and start

again before dusk. It's safer to travel in the dark. Here's some water." Sophie turned her head, and Luther filled her open mouth from a bag.

I'll kill him if the A-Eye don't. And if they haven't killed me first.

Kendella had changed from her work jumper into a dark brown tunic and leggings, better for hiding...and fighting.

"Everyone, this is my mom, Kendella. Everybody calls her K." Ruby, Frenz, and Kendella had just walked up to the clinic. The rest of the group was waiting for them, loaded with bags of food and water. Dawn had just broken through the clouds; pale yellow light touched the tops of the trees around the plaza.

"Nice to meet you, K," said Jen. "And thanks for helping us out. Our girl, Sophie, is precious to us, and we've got to get her back. This will involve some danger...for all of us. The more help we have, the less likely it will be someone gets hurt. Do you have any weapons? Did you bring them?"

"I've got these." Opening her backpack, she pulled out two ancient revolvers, pitted, the bluing long gone. "They look like crap but work just fine. I've got fourteen buddets."

Jen visibly brightened. "Wonderful. I hope we won't need them but am glad you've got them. I don't know how much Ruby or Frenz have told you about this…mission…but we can clear up any questions you have on the way. Ruby knows where the A-Eye congregate, and I suppose you do too."

"Yeah, I do. If that's where we're going, we can get you there. It'll take two days of hard walking, but we know shortcuts that will save us time. Do we have everything we need, supply-wise?"

"We do," said Jen.

"Then let's hit it," Kendella said. With Ruby and Kendella leading the way, they struck out on the widest path through the City toward the foothills.

It was now full-on dark, but the mist had abated. Jen and Frenz worked their way to the front of the line near Ruby and Kendella, who were deep in conversation. For Jen, it was an opportunity to fill Kendella in on the trek from the village to see Albright and Luther's crazed obsession with the A-Eye. For Frenz, it was a chance to watch Kendella walk.

Kendella had questions about Luther, the kidnapping, and Barth's shooting. Jen answered them all. At last, they walked in silence on the wet path.

"Ruby told me you discovered the power plant and how to run it," said Frenz. He'd walked up alongside Kendella.

"Yeah. Took some time to find and understand how it worked, how it *could* work. I found a library that had a book—you know what that is?—with instructions on how to start and maintain the plant. It produces what's called 'hydroelectric power' and was sitting on the south side of the City beneath the dam. We still haven't benefited from everything it can do for us, but it's a start."

"How long have you been managing the plant?"

"Almost twenty years—something like that. Once I found it, I had to get it up and running. That took a year, but I had help. Managing the plant changed our lives—Ruby's and mine—though. I'd had her young, and this work has given me a way to provide for her. That, and much more." Beside him, Kendella looked at Frenz. *Handsome man.*

Frenz was quiet for several minutes. "And her father? Where is he?"

After a moment, Kendella said, "Killed by A-Eye when she was little. Ruby never knew him."

"I'm sorry. I know what that's like, losing someone."

"You have a family?" asked Kendella.

"*Had* a family. That was long ago."

25

A dull light shone through the translucent plassik box. *Something* was in there, but what? Albright ran his hands over the box's corners, all of them. Smooth. Perhaps Luther had been right, and this was sealed with some sort of advanced tech available only at NORAD. The North American Aerospace Defense Command was on the forefront of military technology at The Before's end, so on one level, that made sense. Or was all that talk just more lies from the charlatan? Albright's intuition had been right—as it usually was. The man was a schemer and a criminal. How did he even know about NORAD, and did the box really have anything to do with it? Once Luther had gotten directions and the map to the A-Eye, he'd been more than happy to leave it with Albright.

Albright's intuition told him what was in the box could be important to his lifelong inquiry into Hisry. It might not solve the riddle of the end of The Before or answer the question about where the A-Eye came from, but it might open a fresh line of investigation. He'd had a few of those openings, especially after he'd found the microfilm cache and the reader.

While so far he'd found nothing directly related to whatever happened, he'd found enough about the events of the period to draw a rough sketch of what *could* have happened. There had been wars and rumors of wars worldwide. What wasn't clear was who the principal aggressors were, but they were human. Like everyone else, he knew the stories about things from space starting it all, but that didn't appear to be the case. That didn't rule out, however, some part A-Eye might have played and how that could be connected to beings from another world. Maybe what was in the box would tie everything together. First, he had to open it.

Long ago Albright had asked himself, "Why?" What would finding the cause of the end of The Before mean? Would it change anything? Might it somehow lead to bringing back The Before like Luther hoped? He and Luther were on similar paths; they just had radically different ways of approaching the question. "Commune with the A-Eye" is what Luther said he would do. To what end, exactly? The man was clearly unbalanced. It sounded like his relationship with the man he called "the Prophet" had twisted his mind. He was a fool, but for that matter, so were Jen and her group, thinking they could save the girl Luther had kidnapped. Really? If Luther found the A-Eye, and she was with him, they'd have to walk into the nest to save her!

Albright set the box on the table and brought the light closer to it. What was in the box was a blue-green flat object. That, at least, was clear. Three edges were a lighter color. Beyond that, the plassik—and yes, he was sure it was plassik—obscured detail. *How can I open this?*

Two crossbows, two antique revolvers, fourteen buddets, and eight knives; that's what the six of them carried to take on the one-handed man. Against the A-Eye, though, they had nothing. This "mission" had all the makings of a disaster if they faced the A-Eye. Best case, they'd find Luther, overpower him, free the girl, and hightail it back to the City without ever encountering the A-Eye. Best case.

"How did you come to be part of this group?" asked Kendella. She'd drifted back to walk alongside Frenz, who'd taken Barth's place as the rear guard. Starting out, the trail was tight; they had to squeeze through the boulders in single file. Once in the foothills, however, the way opened. They were headed east, away from the route the villagers had come by.

"Big Rod and I were on our way to the City. After

a few years on the plain, we needed a change, a fresh start. We'd just gotten into the foothills and found Jen, Barth, and Markus. Barth had been shot, and they were stranded. Luther—Jen told you about him, yes? —had kidnapped Sophie. We couldn't leave them where we'd found them, so we helped them to the City. Barth could barely walk; it took a while." Frenz glanced at Kendella. "So here we are."

Kendella nodded. *Good man.* "Was Sophie, the girl, traveling with one of you? Is she married, have a partner?"

"No, although she and Markus seem to be a couple. I don't know all their history, so it's hard to say. They grew up together is all I know."

"You and Big Rod lived on the plain... scavenging?"

"Yeah. He and I are what's left of a band of us. After the A-Eye killed Capper, one of our guys, we decided we'd had enough of the plain and headed to the City. Hoping to find something better, different."

"It was a hard life, I'd imagine."

"You'd be right about that." Frenz glanced at Kendella again. She had beautiful green eyes. "And you? Have you always lived in the City?"

"I have. It's all I've ever known. Once I found the power plant and Louis and I got it up and running, I've never had a reason to leave. Plus, I've got Ruby. Since she's gotten older, she's gotten to be even more of a handful. She's impetuous, willful, and resents everything I try to do for her. You've seen what she's done to her beautiful face? All her friends—she calls them her tribe—did that. I don't understand why… You have children?"

"Once, yes."

Kendella put her hand on his arm. "I'm sorry, Frenz."

With the sun at its zenith, they stopped to eat and drink. Ruby and Kendella bickered about how far it was to the A-Eye nest. The A-Eye had congregated in this spot for years. No one was sure why. Most thought it was where they went to repair themselves; some believed they spawned new A-Eye there. How that was possible was unclear.

After yesterday's rain, the weather had cooled, but the closer they got to the plain, the warmer it got, at least during the day. After much discussion, and after Ruby and K had agreed about how far it was to the nest, they decided to walk until dusk, then camp for the night. The following dawn would put them within striking distance of the A-Eye nest. If they were lucky, they'd reach Luther and Sophie before that. No one wanted to confront the A-Eye.

At the bottom of one of the larger craters, Frenz built a fire. Kendella roasted fresh chicken parts and various vegetables. That, along with loaves from the bakeries, provided a goodly feast. They even had a jug of punkinberry wine from a winery, not that there was cause for celebration. If they had to confront the A-Eye, this could be their last supper.

As night closed, Jen yawned and said she was done for the day. It was strange, her going to bed without Barth near, but Big Rod pulled that duty and stretched out near the fire not far from her. Jen lay thinking about Albright while Big Rod droned on about life scavenging on the plain, finally lulling her to sleep. Frenz and Kendella sat up, whispering into the night on the other side of the fire. As they talked, she found herself more at ease with him. Scavengers were notorious opportunists and couldn't be trusted; somehow, though, she felt he'd opened up honestly to her. His past was still painful for him, but for that matter, so was hers. She fell asleep next to him, wondering.

"Want to find our own crater?" asked Ruby. "There's a small one we passed back there."

"Sure." Markus gathered their water bags, sleeping duffels, and what was left of the wine. They sidestepped up the side of the crater, leaving the fire below. The sky had cleared; the stars were crystal bright.

"Here," said Ruby, pointing. "Right here." They stepped down into a shallow crater. The bottom was flat and small, but there was enough room for the two of them to stretch out.

"Do we need a fire? I have my firestarter, and we can find some scrub."

"We'll be okay," Ruby responded as she smoothed

out the two sleeping duffels, hers and his. She lay down on her back. Glittering stars canopied overhead.

Markus lay down on his side facing her, head propped on an elbow. His dark hair curled on her arm. He studied her profile, so different from Sophie's. *She* was so different from Sophie. "Would you like some of the wine?"

She turned to look at him, dark eyes gleaming in the starlight. "That's not what I want."

Ruby took his hand and put two fingers in her mouth, rolling her tongue around them. She put his hand inside her open tunic and parted her long, outstretched legs. He leaned toward her, nuzzled her neck, then kissed her ear. He reached for her belt.

Markus would remember this night for the rest of his life.

26

They'd walked through the clear moonlit night. Luther directed Sophie, hands tied before her, through the boulder-strewn landscape. Now that the sun had begun to rise, the reds, yellows, and browns of the boulders became clearer, so different from the green of the City. It was jarring.

As the sun rose, Luther called a halt, pointing to a bit of shade beside a boulder. He untied her hands and told her to tie her ankles, which she did. They split rabbit jerky and one of the loaves he'd stolen. When they finished, he retied her, hand and foot, and set her on the ground against the boulder.

"According to Albright's map, we're near the A-Eye. I'll get a little sleep and then scout their camp. You get some rest too, Sophie. Today will be glorious! You'll see. You'll see."

Sophie lay in what little shadow there was beside

the boulder. *Glorious? The fool. He'll get us both killed. I don't know what his plan is—if he even has a plan. I'm either bait or a shield, neither one good. Gods help me!* She lay there full of worry while Luther snored.

The sun climbed higher and around its zenith, Luther rose. Jostling Sophie, he said, "I'll be back. Going to get the lay of the land, so to speak. You stay put!" This always made him laugh. He disappeared between the boulders and was gone.

Two things. Two things I'll do if I get out of this. First, I'll kill him if the A-Eye don't. Then I'll tell Markus how I feel about him. Owen was right: I love him. I guess I always have. Even Jen knew that.

Luther walked down one hill, wound around another, and came to the crown of a taller one topped with boulders. On the hill's crest, he crouched behind one. There, across from and below him, was the A-Eye nest. It was in a large flat-bottomed depression in the side of a hill. Not a canyon exactly, it looked like it might have been made by one of the bombs. Standing in the gloom in the back were the A-Eye, more than a dozen of them. They stood motionless, just as Luther had seen them the afternoon Isabella had been killed, and he'd lost his hand. Was this all of them? Probably not, but it was enough to parlay with. He watched for a time, then started back to where he'd left Sophie.

After a cold late breakfast, Frenz asked Ruby to take him to the A-Eye camp. To avoid them, he needed to know exactly where they were. Before long, they'd climbed a low hill and were hidden behind a scattering of boulders overlooking the A-Eye. Even from a distance, Frenz could smell them. He shuddered at the memory of losing Mutt and Pisser…and Capper.

After a few minutes, Frenz said, "If we all split up and spread out before Luther gets here—form a net between Luther and the A-eye—we've got a good chance of grabbing him. If there's a way to avoid *this*, we'd best take it." Slowly, they backed down from the hilltop and headed back to the others.

Ruby heard Luther first, muttering on the way back to his camp. She tugged Frenz's arm, and they hid as Luther walked a dozen meters in front of them. They watched him pass, then rose to follow. "He was watching the A-Eye camp too," whispered Frenz. "He's on his way back to get Sophie."

Luther kept muttering…and led them to her, tied up in the shadow of a boulder. They snuck as close as they dared and watched as Luther grabbed some bread from a bag and offered Sophie some. "Let's get the others; we'll come back, take him, and get Sophie," whispered Frenz.

They rushed back to camp and Frenz explained: "Luther and Sophie are near here. There are enough of us to surround them. K, give Markus one of your guns and some buddets. Follow me. Quick!"

They hurried to Luther's camp and quietly spread out around it. Frenz and Big Rod had their crossbows, and Kendella and Markus each had one of her revolvers. Jen lifted her walking stick, and Ruby found a hefty rock. At Frenz's signal, they lunged into the camp.

No one was there. Luther and Sophie had left for the A-Eye nest.

As Frenz and Ruby had hastened back to their camp to assemble the rest of the group and their weapons, Luther had roused Sophie; it was time to meet with the A-Eye.

She'd fallen asleep. Untying her legs, he said, "Get up. It's time," leaving her hands tied behind her. She stood awkwardly, yawned, and blinked her eyes awake. *I can't believe he's going through with this. Gods help me!*

Luther stuck his gun in his belt behind him and, with his good arm, guided Sophie through the hills and boulders to the A-Eye nest. She could smell them long before they came into view. As she approached, Luther behind her, she nearly retched. The stink was hideous. They stood motionless toward the back of an open pit, huge, mud-colored, and spotted with small knobs and tubes. Sophie stared in disbelief. A-Eye.

Luther led her slowly down to the cluster of them.

They didn't move. Holding her arm, he marched her forward and pushed her in front of the nearest one, jerking her to a stop.

From above, Frenz, Kendella, Jen, Markus, Ruby, and Big Rod watched from a hill. They'd been too late to stop Luther. All they could do was wait until what lay before them played out; there was no way they could take on the A-Eye.

Clutching Sophie in front of him like a shield, Luther began gesturing, talking. The A-Eye never moved. From a distance, the observers couldn't understand what he was saying, but he was clearly agitated. Waving his arms, he began yelling and shouting and then pushed Sophie into the creature in front of him. She fell into one of its arms as she went down. It reached for her with its other hand cluster.

Jen stood, throwing her walking stick to the ground. "No!" she shouted. Without warning, she ran from the hilltop down the slope to the A-Eye. "Let her be! Leave her alone!"

"Jen!" Big Rod grabbed his crossbow and ran downhill after her as fast as his bandy legs would carry him. He was halfway to her when one of the A-Eye turned to him and fired. A green bolt of fire struck him head-on, and he fell into a heap of black ash and bone. Jen turned to look back in horror, stumbled, and fell to the ground. Sophie screamed.

Markus leaped up and ran from the hilltop past Big Rod's smoking remains to Sophie and Jen. He shoved Luther to the ground, took Sophie's arm and pulled her upright, grabbed Jen, and hauled both back up the hill. Aside from the single blast at Big Rod, the A-Eye never stirred.

Stunned, Luther scrambled to his feet and fled.

27

"Thank the gods!" Jen was shaking with relief. "We thought we'd lost you." She hugged Sophie tightly. They all did, even Kendella and Ruby.

"You're safe now. You're safe," said Markus, grasping Sophie's hand. They had retreated from the A-Eye camp to a sheltered place behind a group of boulders with red, brown, and white stripes. The air still stank.

"What a nightmare," said Sophie. "What happened to Luther? Where did he go?"

"He ran off," said Markus. "The A-Eye didn't stop him."

"And who was killed? Who was that?" Sophie eagerly guzzled the water offered to her.

Frenz nodded. "My partner, Big Rod. He ran to save Jen…and you. He had his crossbow, and the A-Eye must have seen him as a threat." Frenz paused, eyes focused elsewhere. "He didn't deserve that. He was a good man, a loyal man."

Jen nodded, "Yes, he was. A very good man."

"I'm so sorry. And who are you?" asked Sophie, looking at Frenz.

"Sophie, these are our new friends," explained Markus. "This is Frenz. He and Big Rod found us in the foothills after Barth was shot and helped us to the City. And this is Kendella and her daughter, Ruby. They live in the City and know Albright. They led us here to find you. Without all of them, this would have turned out very differently."

"Thank you. Thank all of you." Sophie shook all of their hands. "Do you have any food? I'm famished. Luther was not a good host." For the first time, she smiled.

"Of course," said Jen, laughing. "Let's move up the trail, find a place to sit, and get away from that stink."

They found a sheltered area between boulders, sat, and ate and drank. Sophie couldn't take her eyes off Ruby. She'd never seen anyone like her. "Did what happened to your face hurt?" she asked.

Ruby bristled, touching the scars on her cheeks. "No. I did it myself. It's the mark of our tribe."

"Tribe?"

"Yes. Those I belong to…in the City. We grew up together, support each other. These marks show the world that we are family." Ruby glared at Sophie.

Turning to Jen to change the subject, Sophie asked, "And Barth, where is he? Is he okay?"

"He's not completely healed, but much better," said Jen. "There's a clinic in the City, and he's recovering there. Of course he wanted to join us, but I insisted he stay there; he's still weak. Sophie, he'll be so glad to see you! So much has happened since we last saw you. We found Albright and tried to catch Luther but he escaped. You won't believe the things the City has. In some ways, it's like our village, but they have shops and *power*. Electricity!" Jen looked at Kendella and smiled. "I'm so glad you're safe!"

"I can't wait to see it all," Sophie said, digging into her bread and jerky.

With Kendella leading the way, they walked through the foothills. Frenz was following her when his head jerked. He threw up a hand to stop and grabbed Kendella's arm.

He smelled it. They all smelled it: the rotted stench of the A-Eye that stepped in front of them from behind an enormous boulder.

Frenz pulled his crossbow behind him. Everyone stood still. The thing stepped forward past Kendella and into their midst, its sensory tubes pulsing. The "head" turned, and it stepped to stand in front of Ruby. She gagged.

With one arm, it scooped her up around the

waist, binding her arms to her body. Kendella screamed as the A-Eye stomped off. "My baby! No!" she wailed.

They all stood in stunned silence, then Markus shouted at Frenz, "Follow me." The two of them slid around boulders and disappeared down the hillside. They ran parallel to the A-Eye as it made its way to its camp, gaining ground until they were several hundred meters in front of it.

Panting, Markus stopped. "If you can distract it, I'll grab Ruby." They'd stopped beside a boulder twice as tall as either of them. "Frenz, can you climb up there," he said, pointing, "and hit it with something? Something to knock it down or over so I can grab her? How big a rock can you manage?"

"Help me, and we'll get one up there big enough to do some damage. You'll still only have a second to get her. I just need to make sure I don't hit her."

Frenz stepped from foothold to foothold up the side of the boulder. Halfway up, he gestured for Markus to hand up the large red and brown rock. Together, they got it to the top. Frenz crouched low, balancing the rock on the edge. Markus moved into the boulder's shadow.

They smelled it again, stronger, that stench. The tinny mechanical sound grew louder, as did Ruby's protests. The A-Eye lumbered down the path, holding her as she squirmed and yelled. As it walked below Frenz, he pushed the rock over the edge. It landed on the back of the A-Eye's stubby head and knocked its sensory tubes askew.

The A-Eye threw up both arms, hand clusters feeling for the wrecked tubes. Ruby dropped to the ground as Markus charged from the shadow and pulled her from beneath the creature, grabbing her hand. They sprinted back up the hill, dodging between rocks. Frenz scuttled down from the boulder and ran the other way. The A-Eye floundered in circles as it tried to locate its damaged sensory tubes.

Ruby was shaken but unharmed. "Thank the gods… again," said Jen. They spent a minute warmly embracing Ruby, all of them.

"Let's save the congratulations for later. That A-Eye is still out there, and we don't want to push our luck. It'll be dark in a couple of hours," said Frenz.

"Thank you," Ruby whispered to Markus. He hugged her tightly, his arm around her waist. "I wasn't going to lose you," he said. Sophie stared at them.

Kendella had said little since the A-Eye marched off with Ruby. Frenz went to her. "K, are you okay? She's safe now," he said. He wrapped his arms around her, and she hugged him tightly.

She looked up at him, tears in her eyes. "We fight, we disagree, and she drives me crazy sometimes, but I don't know what I'd do without her. She's all I have in the world. It's all been on me since she was born. Her father's never shown love for her, never been there for her…or me. All Albright cares about is his lab and those damned A-Eye. It's all been on me. All of it. Always."

Jen had been following them and heard every word. Her mouth dropped open.

28

That bitch! Luther was steamed. *I had them. They were ready to parlay. I know it. I was this close! Then she butts in and...ruins it. I'll kill that brown bitch. It should have been her the A-Eye burned, not the runt. I'd kill them all if I had enough ammunition. At least Sophie is finally off my hands. What a nightmare she turned out to be. Another bitch!*

After escaping the fiasco with the A-Eye, Luther circled back to the camp where he and Sophie had rested before heading to the A-Eye. He'd left water there and a little food, enough to get him back to the City. He grabbed what he needed—which was every-thing—and started back through the foothills, not sure of exactly where he was going.

Whichever way they went, they'll pass between the red rocks on the way back. I can be there and snuff that bitch, Jen, and as many of the others as I can. He checked his revolver.

Kendella said little on the way back to the City. She and Frenz walked side by side when the path was wide enough. Frenz glanced at her when he could, trying to gauge whether he should say anything to brighten her spirits. She was a strong woman—he knew that—but Ruby's abduction had shaken her.

At a wide spot in the path, he stepped aside and pulled her after him, looking into her beautiful eyes. "K, she's all right. She's safe. She doesn't know it or show it, but you're the best thing that will ever happen to her. She's lucky to have you as a mom. We'll get you both back to the City, and all of this will be over. Promise."

Kendella leaned against him. "I hope so."

As she walked behind them, Sophie continued to watch Markus and this new strange woman. *What's going on? He had his arm around her, and she snuggled up to him. Was she just showing her gratitude or... And he hasn't said five words to me? I don't understand.*

Markus and Ruby walked together along the path, chatting amiably. Occasionally she'd put her hand on his shoulder, like they were the oldest of friends.

What was that business about being in a tribe? Is that a City thing? Surely, he doesn't find those scars on her face attractive. It's like he's someone else, not the Markus I know. Not my Markus.

They walked for two more hours and found a place beside the path to camp for the night. At dusk, water bags were passed around along with loaves and jerky. K pulled out fruit she'd brought. Everyone got a bite or two for dessert. Frenz built a fire, and they settled in for the evening. Ruby and Markus drifted off by themselves. K and Frenz sat near the fire talking. Sophie looked for Jen and found her sitting at the edge of the firelight.

"Jen, can I talk to you for a minute?" Jen sat against a rock, her knees drawn up to her chin, eyes downcast.

"What? Oh. Sure, Sophie." She patted the space beside her and Sophie sat.

"Who's the new girl, Ruby? What's with her and Markus? He's hardly spoken to me."

"To be honest…I think she's…well, she's all over him. I'm afraid he's fallen under her spell, if you will. I wish I could tell you that's not so, but what you've seen is the way it is."

"Oh."

"I'm so sorry, Sophie. I've always thought you and Markus would be…together, a couple, more than just friends. I thought that was happening. Then this girl, Ruby, swooped in and grabbed Markus's attention. She's interesting, no doubt, but I don't know what she wants from Markus. I know what he's getting from her, though."

Sophie's eyes teared up. "Oh." She was quiet for

several minutes. "I thought so too…that we'd become —I don't know—partners, start a family, that finding the plassik box and this trip would change everything for us, make all that possible. I've had so much time to think about Markus…I love him, I always have, but didn't know that's what it was. I told myself if I got out of the mess with Luther, I'd tell Markus how I felt. Now…"

Jen put her arm around Sophie and pulled her to her. "Not everything we hope for comes to pass, Sophie. This I know."

"Markus, can I ask you something?" Ruby and Markus had slipped away to a shallow crater nearby. They lay bundled up against the pending chill.

"Of course."

"Jen told me you and Sophie grew up together, have been together all your lives. Didn't sound like you were a 'thing,' but the way you ran down to save her…" She looked Markus in the eye. "I want you to tell me the truth. Was that because you love her or because it was the right thing to do? I just want to know."

"Ruby, I've told you I've been confused about how I feel about Sophie. She's been my best friend since we were kids. I couldn't, won't, let anything happen to her. But that's not the same as loving her."

"And what about me? How do you feel about me?"

Markus was silent for a minute. "I've never known anyone like you. I've never *wanted* anyone like you. I see you, and I see a future I couldn't imagine when I lived in the village. I knew this trip would bring changes...the box and all that, Luther, Albright. All this is new to me, but the newest, most exciting thing, Ruby, is you. You." He took her in his arms.

They started early for the City the next day. Jen didn't seem to have the energy she had had, so Frenz and Kendella took the lead, pushing to get to the clinic to check on Barth and see if Albright had found a way to open the plassik box. They made good time.

Red Rock Pass was a signpost for travelers to the City coming from the foothills. It signaled the outskirts lay not far ahead. As red as the name implied, the rocks were tall and easily seen. The group wound single file through the pass, boulders looming above them. At some points, it was so narrow they had to lift their bundles above their heads to slip through.

"I'll be ready for a bath," said Sophie. "I'm so ready to wash Luther's madness off me. Ugh!"

"You'll get that soon enough," said Jen. "And a proper meal too. Maybe we can even find more of that wine and have a real celebration."

Luther stepped out from behind a red boulder after the rest had passed, waving his gun. "You! Bitch!"

Jen turned, surprised, and raised her hand as if to fend him off. Luther leveled his revolver, shot her in the chest, and ran. The screaming started.

29

Frenz and Markus fashioned a litter out of poles and strips cut from empty water bags. They laid Jen on it and carried her through the pass and out of the foothills. Kendella had cleaned and dressed her wound, and for most of the time, Jen was unconscious. Frenz had restocked his medpack after Barth's injury and gave Jen a sleeping powder to ease her pain. Now all they could do was hope they would get her to the clinic in time. When Frenz and Markus tired, Ruby and Kendella carried the litter. Once they got into the forest surrounding the City and onto the wider beaten path to the plaza, the way became easier.

Their luck changed for the better as a two-wheeled cart pulled up behind them. At its jingling bells, Ruby turned around. "Oy! Are you headed to the plaza?" she asked. Two Loca women, one young, one elderly but fit, pulled the cart.

"That we are. Looks like you could use some help with that," said the elder of the two, nodding at Jen. "What's happened here?"

"Gunshot. Need to get her to the clinic," said Frenz. "Can you help us?"

"Of course." The cart had stopped. "Load her on the back. You can keep her on the litter. There are ropes to tie it in place."

Markus and Frenz slid the litter onto the back of the cart, tying it down. "If you'd like, we can take over the hauling," said Markus. "Be happy to."

While holding the cart level, he and Frenz stepped into the cart harnesses and leaned forward, starting down the path at a faster clip than the two Loca.

Walking alongside Ruby, the older woman asked, "What happened? You say it was a gunshot? Don't hear of those much. Is she okay?"

"We hope so."

Shade along the path helped all of them revive a bit, and soon they were in front of the clinic. Kendella ran to the door while Markus and Frenz untied the litter. "Owen? Owen?" she called. He came to the door, wiping his hands. Two Loca had heard him yelling for help, found him in the forest, and helped him back to the clinic.

"Jen's been shot!"

Barth appeared behind Owen at the mention of Jen's name. "What? Jen?" he roared; he pushed Owen aside and hobbled outside. Markus and Frenz slid the litter from the cart, marched inside with it, and, at Owen's direction, slipped Jen off and onto a cot.

"Good god!" Owen said. "How long ago did this happen? Who did this? Not Luther, I hope."

"Two days ago, and yes, it was Luther," answered Markus. "It's a long story."

"Well, step aside, all of you, and let me get to work. Jen, can you hear me?"

There was nothing any of them could do but fret while Owen tended to Jen. Occasionally he'd give them a bit of news: "The buddet missed her lung, but she's lost a lot of blood," and later, "Looks like it made a clean exit." To free up space for Owen to work, they'd all, including Barth, moved out to the fountain in the plaza. The day was waning when a boy from the clinic came to them and said, "Barth, Jen would like to see you."

Barth limped into the clinic.

Owen pulled up a chair beside Jen and pointed Barth toward it. He sat.

Jen did not look good. Her hair was matted with dried sweat, and her face was the color of walnuts. She lay on her back. Barth leaned in to hear what she had to say.

"I've got to check on the plant," said Kendella, rising from the fountain's wall. "Want to come?"

Frenz shook his head. "No, Jen's in worse shape than I thought. You go on; I'll stay here."

Barth came out of the clinic and walked toward them, stopping in front of Sophie. "Sophie, she wants to see you." Sophie glanced at Markus and walked into the clinic. Owen met her and, taking her arm, said, "She's very weak, so please don't tire her. I'll be nearby if she needs me."

Sophie moved to Barth's chair and sat. "Jen, how are you? It's Sophie."

Jen's eyes were closed but opened at the sound of Sophie's voice. "Oh, Sophie. Thank you." She spoke just above a whisper.

"Sophie, the time will come when you know your life is ending."

Sophie's eyes widened.

"That time for me is very near, and I'm okay with that. There's one thing, though, I have to take care of: the village. Being its leader, even having it called 'Jen's Place,' has not been easy. One of my responsibilities —one I thought was far in the future—is to name my successor, someone to take my place." She took Sophie's hand and looked up at her. "And that person is you, Sophie."

Sophie sat open-mouthed. "Me? No, Jen, I can't…"

"Oh, Sophie, yes you can. You're more than capable and ready to do this. It's hard to see ourselves, who we are, who we can be. I've known you since you were young, and I know this about you: your strength and compassion will carry you into the wisdom it takes to lead a group of people, people who will need you, people who will love you. Your people in the village."

"But Jen…"

"I've spoken with Barth. He'll see you back to the woodland and announce that you are my chosen successor. He'll be by your side as he has been at mine."

"But I don't know how…"

"There's only one piece of advice I can give you, Sophie, and that's to take care of what's in front of you. That's all."

Sophie placed her hand on top of Jen's. "If you believe I can do this, I will, Jen. I'll do it for you. And for the village."

"Good. Now I have another favor to ask. Please find Albright and bring him to me."

Albright's work on the plassik box had paid off. Using an electrically powered saw, he split one of the sides.

All that remained was cutting a flapped opening wide enough to get out whatever was inside. The plassik itself was valuable and so far, hadn't been damaged enough to change that.

Sophie found her way to the Hilto, rushed inside, and found Albright at his table.

"Jen's been shot. She's in the clinic and wants to see you. Right now."

Albright turned from his work, puzzled. "Shot?"

"Yes. That lunatic Luther shot her when we were in the foothills. We just got her back to the clinic. She's not doing well."

He rose from his chair, set the saw and box on a table, and headed to the door. "How bad is she?"

"She thinks she's dying."

Together they hustled to the clinic. Albright found Owen and pulled him aside in an alcove. "Owen, how bad is she?"

"She was shot in the chest. The buddet passed through, but she's lost a great deal of blood. It's touch and go. She wants to see you. Make it quick."

Albright sat by the cot. Jen looked terrible. "Jen. Jen, it's me."

She opened her eyes. "Albright? You came. Thank you."

"I'm so sorry you've been hurt, Jen. What can I do?"

"Not much *to* do, I'm afraid. Not to worry,

though. But let's not talk about that. I want to talk about us."

"Us?"

"Albright, I didn't say it then, but I'm saying it now. I love you. I loved you when we were young, back in the village, but didn't say it. It's the biggest regret of my life, but now…now I've finally made that right." She winced. "Tell me. Did you love me?"

Albright said nothing for a moment. "Jen, I was a coward…and stupid. My work became the most important thing to me. I thought you'd be in the way of it, but that when I was done, I'd find you and we'd… but the work was never done. I learned to live with that, thinking about a future that I let slip away. I've never stopped thinking about you. Yes, I loved you. I still love you." He took her hand in both of his and drew closer, the silver moon necklace resting on her arm. "Can you forgive me for my arrogance? And stupidity?"

"Of course. We were both fools, young fools. Albright, there's something else. You have a daughter with K. Ruby is your child, yes?" He nodded. "Don't do to her what you did to me. Don't shut her out. Be the father she needs, she's always needed. She doesn't know you're her father, does she?"

Albright shook his head. "No, she believes her father died when she was very young. It was easier that way…for me…than to… I cut them both out of my life, Ruby and K. I was selfish."

"Don't let her slip away. It's not too late. You can still be there for her. Will you do that? Do that for me, be the father to the daughter we never had?"

"Yes. I can do that."

Jen smiled, closed her eyes, and was still.

30

In the downstairs gloom of the power plant, turbines hummed and gauges flicked back and forth. Kendella and Frenz sat at a corner of her desk, a long affair that had once been a door. She was off duty—Louis was managing things upstairs—and wore a dark blue tunic and gray leggings. Her short hair was brushed back. She was a handsome woman.

"I've got to hand it to you, K; this is something, this whole operation." Frenz swept his hands at the machinery. "Hats off to you for resurrecting it."

"All it took was time and reference books," she said. "I had help too. Louis has been my right-hand man from the beginning. He and others got excited once it looked like it could actually work. I wanted you to see all this, Frenz, and to tell you something. I wanted to explain about Albright and Ruby."

"No need. Things happen."

"No, I wanted you to know why Ruby never knew Albright was her father. Why we—I—kept that from her, let her think her father was dead. Part of me regrets that decision, but after watching Albright all these years, I know I did the right thing. He would never have been a good father. His work always absorbed him; all he's ever cared about has been his search for Hisry. When we got together, after he first got here—I was young, and you've seen him; he's magnetic—it just happened."

Kendella paused. "I'm telling you this because I don't want you to think I'm a bad person or conniving. I like you, Frenz, really like you. You know that." She leaned forward and touched his arm. "I think you might like me too, maybe more than that. I don't know what your plans are now, but...I'd like for you to stay here, in the City."

Frenz rubbed his beard. "K, I don't know if I can. I don't know if I know how...to be with someone. It's been...too long since I've had anyone close in my life...except for a bunch of no-counts." He smiled the smallest smile, the wrinkles around his eyes sharper. "When I lost my family, I...dried up. Nothing seemed to matter anymore. It's been so long..."

Kendella sighed. "Frenz, we're more alike than you know. I've been alone for a long time too. This job and Ruby have been my life, but they can't be all there is for me. You're a good man. I've seen that, and

I'm ready to try again, to love someone and be loved. I think you are too. I hope you are."

Frenz looked past her. "After I'd been scavenging for a while, I ended up the leader of a pack of five men. We lived together, scavenged together. By the time we made it here, it was just Big Rod and me. I've lost them all, just like I lost my family. K, I don't know if I can be trusted to protect anyone who depends on me."

"I'm not looking for protection, Frenz. I'm looking for a partner. All I ask is that you think about it." She took his hand in hers.

"I will," he said.

Markus, Sophie, Frenz, Kendella, and Ruby sat on the edge of the dry fountain watching the clinic. When the dark figure of Albright walked out, they knew Jen had passed. His shoulders slumped, and his dreadlocks hung like old wash. Grief poured from him.

"I'm so sorry," said Sophie. "I know what she must have meant to you because I know what you meant to her. Even if she never told you." Albright looked up at her. He said nothing.

They all sat in silence for a few minutes. After all they'd been through, *this* was the most unexpected. For the villagers, Jen was the beating heart of their lives, had always been there. For the rest—Frenz,

Ruby, Kendella—she'd earned their respect and affection. Now she was gone.

"She asked me to take her place as leader of the village," Sophie said softly, glancing at Markus.

"And what did you say?"

"I said I would. How could I not? She was a mother to me. If she believes I can lead her people, I can and I will. I owe her that much. No one can replace her, but I can carry her legacy forward as best I can. Barth and I will go back to the village as soon as possible. I know Jen would like to be buried there, but I don't know if we can carry her back across the plain."

Markus said nothing.

"We can get her ready if that's what you plan on doing," said Kendella. "It won't be an easy trip, but it can be done. If that's what she would have wanted…"

Barth limped out of the clinic, his head hung as he walked to the fountain. There was nothing to be said to him. In the early afternoon cool, clouds had gathered, the wind shifting. Did the universe feel Jen's loss?

Albright straightened and cleared his throat. "I'm going back to the Hilto. I've made headway with the box. If anyone would like to come…" Those on the fountain wall hopped off and followed Albright and Barth. All except Sophie and Markus.

After they left, Sophie turned to Markus. "Markus, I was hoping you'd come back to the village with me and Barth. If we bring Jen's body, we'll need all the help we can get."

Markus couldn't look her in the eye. "I'm staying here, Sophie." He shifted to face her but still didn't look her in the eye. "When we talked about the future, what this trip could mean for us, we had no idea all this would happen. I knew things would change, but I never saw any of this coming: your kidnapping, Jen getting shot. Ruby."

"Ruby. That's what this is about, isn't it? I'm not blind, Markus. I just…I just don't understand how it could have happened so fast. You and I have been together all our lives and in an instant you…what… love her?" She touched his arm. "Do you love her, Markus?"

Now he looked her in the eye. "I can't explain what it is, but it's something, someone, I want. You'll always be closer to me than anyone. How can you not be? But I can't miss this, this thing I feel. All of a sudden, the world has opened up. Everything is possible." He looked away. "I'm staying here with Ruby. I'm sorry, Sophie."

Sophie looked at the clinic and said nothing for a moment. "All right. Jen told me once that what we want isn't always what we need. Maybe it's time, and this is what growing up is. For both of us." She dropped off the fountain wall, dusted off her gray shift, and walked toward the clinic, not looking back. "I've got things to take care of."

Dark had come to the City. Parts were glowing with light from electric bulbs. The rest was deep blue softened only by the occasional fire or candle. Inside the Hilto, Albright and Markus worked on the box.

Barth stood beside them at the worktable. For the first time since Jen's death, he spoke. "I had a vision. About this moment." He told them about seeing a man with the box, illuminated by a strange candle, about the man holding something up, something from the box. "I couldn't see what it was, but he acted like it was important. Very important."

The electric saw screamed against the side of the box and soon a flap appeared. Albright pried it open, slipped his long fingers into the box, and pulled out what was inside.

It was blue green, a little less than an inch thick and made of paper. It was a book, or what would have been called a manual. Albright took it to the light. He read the cover, then flipped through the pages, stopping now and again to study one and then another more closely. There were diagrams and pages and pages of print.

Albright looked up smiling, eyes clear: "It's instructions on how to disable the A-Eye. It's how to build the kill-switch."

EPILOGUE

Ruby hugged her mother long and hard and acknowledged Albright with a small smile. He'd come to see her off.

"I can't believe you're leaving," said Kendella, "but I'm not surprised." She turned to Markus. "Take care of her, Markus. She's all I've got."

Markus stood by Ruby, holding two well-stuffed bags. Water bags lay at his feet. "She's all I've got too. I'll take care of her. Promise."

"Where will you go?" asked Kendella.

"We know what's west," said Ruby, "the foothills and then the plain. Same as to the east, so we'll follow the river north over the mountains. Don't know what's there, but we'll discover that along the way." She hugged Markus around the waist. He glowed.

"And you, Mom, what about you? What will you do? Will you move back in with Dortiz?"

Kendella laughed and looked at Frenz, who stood beside her. "I think I'll be just fine, Ruby." She took Frenz's hand. They both smiled.

In the end, her friends buried Jen in the Loca cemetery on the outskirts of the City. There she'd be near the one man she'd ever loved. Sophie and Barth stayed until after Jen's service, gathered supplies, and struck out across the plain for the village. Sophie wished Markus and Ruby safe travels, pivoted, and never looked back.

After capturing an A-Eye to test effective options, Albright built the kill-switch and turned off every A-Eye. It was underwhelming; they just stopped in their tracks. Try as he might, he could never with certainty determine who had built the A-Eye. The manual was in English, but that didn't narrow it down much. Luther had said it was somehow connected to NORAD, but neither Markus nor Sophie could confirm that, and they'd been the ones to find the box.

The manual did have some revelations. As suspected, A-Eye were "…autonomous robots whose generative learning has broken through the consciousness barrier and become sentient." They were "cybernetic biomechanical entities that used amino acids to generate internal power." That explained the appetite for meat and their horrible stench. With the manual as a guide, Albright would continue to look for the doorway to The Before.

Regarding the plassik box, before they each left, Sophie and Markus got an advance from Albright for the box's eventual sale to a collector, enough to help cover whatever was next. For Sophie, it was establishing herself as Jen's heir. "The woodland will always be called 'Jen's Place.' I'm just the caretaker." For Markus, it added some security as he and Ruby made their way into their future.

Markus and Ruby headed into the rising sun the day they left. Kendella, Frenz, and Albright came to see them off. What was out there past the mountains? There was only one way to find out.

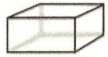

ACKNOWLEDGMENTS

Thanks to my mom who read to me as a child, readying the movie screen in my mind; to Miss Helen Greenwood, my high school English teacher, who showed me that play with words could be fun; to Theodore Sturgeon, Fritz Lieber, Ray Bradbury, John Cheever, H. P. Lovecraft, Philip K. Dick, James Blish, Cordwainer Smith, Charles Bukowski, T. C. Boyle, Connie Willis, William Gibson, Ann Leckie, Malka Older, Octavia Butler, S. D. Divya, Cory Doctorow, and Nnedi Okorafor for inspiring me. Special thanks to Pat Frank who years ago began my trek through apocalyptic landscapes.

And to Chuck Berry, Little Richard, Jimmy Reed, Otis Redding, Wilson Pickett and the Beatles because they rock!

And thanks to you for reading this story about The After!

Thanks to you all.

ABOUT THE AUTHOR

Writers are readers. Ernie's been an avid reader since he was a kid. In elementary school he could order those nifty two-book paperbacks with a novel on one side and a different novel on the other and was drawn to science fiction as it was called in those days, now more broadly known as speculative fiction. The first post-apocalyptic novel he read was Pat Frank's *Alas, Babylon* published in 1959. He was fifteen.

Although he wrote his first science fiction story when he was 12 years old, most of his writing has been as a songwriter. Whether it's a song, a short story or a novel, it's all stories. Truth be told, he prefers writing fiction because it has fewer limitations than a song with its meter, rhyme scheme and phrasing constraints.

As a musician, Ernie has appeared twice on PBS's *Austin City Limits* and is a member of the Texas Songwriters Association Texas Music Legends Hall of Fame. As an artist, he exhibits at art markets around the state. His art, music videos, and writing can be found on his web site, www.ernies-artmusic.com

Author's Note:

If you enjoyed reading *After The Before*, I hope you'll leave a review on Amazon, Goodreads, or any of your favorite readers' or social media sites. And if you'd like to read a sequel to this book, I'd love to know whose story you'd like to follow in The After! Drop me a line at www.ernies-artmusic.com or mention it in your review. Thanks!

ALSO BY ERNIE GAMMAGE

WHAT AWAITS?

(a speculative short fiction collection)